Speak

noelle bodhaine

Naughty Nellies Pervy Press

ISBN-13: 978-0692352939 (Custom)

ISBN-10: 0692352937

CONTENTS

All the thanks would never be enough for the people who helped me along this journey. To you I say my voice was once a whisper but I am learning to speak and when I find my mountain top and shout at the top of my lungs I will be shouting THANK YOU to every single one of you who helped me get to there.

Contributors:

Edited by Colleen LeHew Lee

Formatted by Noelle Bodhaine

Cover Design by Noelle Bodhaine and Tiffany Huegele

noelle bodhaine

SPEAK

You

If you trust in me – my devotion to you
I could then reach in – to the heart of you
Find the shards – that left scars in you
Kiss them hard – they'd be rid of you
Then that's a love – so worthy of you

~ Darcy

Prologue

Three weeks ago I allowed my heart to get broken. I will not make the mistake again. I knew better. But I let myself get swept away, in a moment that lasted too long. I saw only what I wanted, blinded myself to the reality of my place in his world. I was swept up in the force of nature that is Rhys Slate.

Note to self: a society wedding is no place to begin a relationship. There is a reason why the thought of the best man and a bridesmaid is such a cliché, because it is just that, a terrible cliché. How I convinced myself that it could have been anything else is beyond me. I was possessed and defenseless. The way Rhys so effortlessly swept me off of my feet. I think I forgot what it felt like to walk on solid ground, terra firma. I was floating high above it all, wrapped in his strong arms, hypnotized by his sweet words. Ugh. The thought makes me cringe. How easily I folded, how easily he fooled me. But my feet are firmly planted now. Yet even as the numbing anger settles over me, I can still be rocked by tremors that ring from his fingerprints. They are tattooed all over my body, little reminders of how amazing he could make me feel. How thoroughly he rocked my foundations, and how he branded me with his body.

***

"Sophie, are you alright?" I am pulled from my shock by the strained note in Mary's voice. I snap my neck up and look her dead in the eyes, willing myself not to crack. "Should I not have shown you that?" she asks meekly, trying to pry the photo from my white knuckled grip.

"Um…" I am lost, trapped in my head for a moment that drags. Pondering, creating, grasping for any good reason why he would have been with her and not said anything. Thursday, my first night home. He sent me flowers, gardenias. Bile rises in the back of my throat, but I push it back, determined to make it out of here with my dignity and emotions intact. I smile at Mary, as genuinely as I can muster, but she is no fool.

"I'm sorry, Sweetie." She pats my hands, pity welling in her dull blue eyes.

"It's fine," I lie. "It was a few days, right? It's not a big deal. I haven't even seen him since then anyhow." Why was I lying? Self-preservation maybe, I don't know. I just wanted to get out as fast as I could. I needed to be home so I could sort the details and play it all out. I needed to get away from Mary and the pity party she was preparing in my honor. "I am going to finish up at home, OK? Can I take a rain check on lunch?" I ask, trying to sound as nonchalant as possible. I missed the mark totally, by the look on her face. I feel frantic, packing up my things, but I cannot get out of here fast enough. I stop, take a deep breath, smooth my skirt and take Mary's hands in mine. "I am fine, really. It is no big deal. I am just so tired, I had a long night. I really want to go home." She takes me at face value, at least it seems that way. "Send me the link to that article and I will work on it at home." I hug her; grab my purse and turn to go, repeating, "Send me that link."

Moving through shadows in my apartment, I make a beeline to my bedroom. I promised him I wouldn't come back here. But promises mean nothing. I don't know why, but I shut the door behind me, as if to hide some secret, my secretly breaking heart perhaps. I check the window, making sure it is still locked. Climbing on the bed, I fold my legs beneath me and lean heavily on the pillows at my back. This is going to hurt. I open the waiting message from Mary. There it is, the link to my truth. The truth that I have known all along, yet I allowed myself to subscribe to the lie. I am a lie junkie.

Maybe I am overreacting. I slide my finger over the link, and their picture springs to life, practically leaping off the extra large screen, Nadja and Rhys. She stares back at me, her dark eyes and perfect pout mocking every inch of my averageness. And he looks so carefree, so happy, like he does in all the pictures I have seen of him, pictures with other women. What made me think that I mattered to him? Maybe the fact that he said I did. He showed up here, like a white knight. He rescued me from my ex, who was out for blood. He did that. He saved me from Collin, if he and Charlie hadn't showed…. I cannot even fully form the thought. The terrifying thought of what might have happened if he hadn't come. Come unannounced and uninvited. Of course, he wasn't here to rescue me. He was here for a fuck. The thought stings in my head, but rings true. That is what this has always been. Sex. I stare down at the picture until it blurs and swirls in a deluge of uninvited tears. I swipe them away violently, pulling at the delicate skin around my eyes. I tug, and rub, willing the tears to stop when my phone comes to life, the bell tolling for me, a message from Rhys.

I have been thinking about you all day...

I stare at the words and they are hollow. Every second that passes makes those words a bigger lie and a massive insult. The slow simmering anger and sense of betrayal bubbles until it boils over. Deafening white noise roars in my ears, humming over any rational thoughts that may be fighting for supremacy. I am livid, devastated, sad. Livid feels good, the anger fits like a warm coat I can wrap around myself, protection against a cold snap. I choose to focus on the anger, anger at being deceived again, anger at being used again, anger at myself for surrendering so easily. I look down on the words again, but this time all I see is a lie, a lie from a skilled liar. I forward the link to Rhys, no message, no bait.

Watching the ticker swirl until the message has been sent, I stare at the phone. A simple piece of technology, a gift from Rhys, a bridge, he built that flimsy bridge so he could stay in my life. A line to another woman he could use for his own end. Well, I am not that submissive fool that he had, time and time again in Miami. And he has himself to thank for that. I will not be lied to or made a fool of. I am stronger, smarter and out for myself. He has created a monster that he just turned on himself. I stare at the phone, at the message that mocks me. He held me, told me I was better than that. Why did I trust him? Because I was blinded, that's why, by his prowess, his silky words, his body.

Everything changed when he showed up and beat the shit out of Collin. A fundamental shift, a fling turned something more. I told him things I wanted nobody to know. Things I would deny until my dying day, things that paint my soul with the brush of shame and self-loathing. Anger grows deep in my chest, blooming into a thorny, blood-red rose. I will not be a toy. I am going to burn that bridge to the ground! Taking a page from Rhys' book, I dismantle the phone that he gave me, tearing the battery from the back and drop the pieces of his burning bridge onto the bed.

I watch the now quiet, broken technology lay lifeless on the duvet and know that one day I will thank him. Thank him for showing me things about myself I may never have known. But mostly for showing his true colors before my heart got too tangled to escape. What a difference a day makes. This morning, I woke with a glow, feeling safe and hopeful. Tonight I lay alone, in an empty bed, a dark pit growing in my belly, a pit where I will put him and never let him out. I drop the two empty pieces of the phone into my night stand and sit in self-imposed silence, in a purgatory of my own making.

The haste of a broken phone leaves a sour taste in my mouth. But I cannot talk to him, cannot give him a chance to lie his way out of this picture, the write up. My stomach lurches into my throat. The write up, *Powerhouse couple…Society fixture....Wedding Bells....* The words play over in my head, a haunting ticker that keeps coming back around. What was I thinking? How could I have believed that I belonged with him? Belonged, or had even earned a pass into his world, his life. Clearly I was never a part of his life. I was a toy, easily discarded as soon as the shine wore off. Who am I kidding? It was four days in Miami. Four sex-filled days with a man I hardly knew. How did I convince myself that it was anything other than that? I knew when Nadja showed up at the house on Biscayne that something wasn't right. But I pushed it down. I didn't listen to myself. It was all supposed to be so casual.

Anger shifts from Rhys to me. I turn it on myself and the rock solidifies in my gut immediately. I am to blame. I opened the cage. I knew he was trouble from moment one, knew he was out of my league. He is a powerful, wild, rare tiger, with an insatiable appetite. I am an average little field mouse. I opened the cage and walked right in, locked the door behind me, offered myself up on a silver platter, a sweet little meal that he didn't even have to work for, a small forgettable morsel.

Chapter 1

"God Damn It!"

"What is it, Son? Must be serious to call upon God."

"Sorry, Da, just a complication. Have you looked over the financials for Viktor? I am anxious to get this done. Nadja is becoming something of a liability."

"I have, Son, I trust your instincts. If you need to pass it on to your team to wrap it up, then by all means, do so. We have done all we can for him. He dug himself this hole. You owe Viktor nothing." He runs his finger along the rim of his scotch, a habit he has fostered since I can remember. He is waiting, waiting for me to volunteer more information. Tossing back the last finger of scotch, he eyes me with a growing curiosity. "Does your complication have a name?" His fatherly stare shoots straight through me, like only he can. "Come now, Son, I know that look. I have worn that look, more times than I care to remember. Only a woman can provoke a look like that." He is shrewd and dead on. "A man's eyes can only be made hollow by a woman who has stolen his heart." The burn of the scotch reaches my nostrils and I choke at his sentiment.

"It's not as serious as that."

"Isn't it now?" He smirks and raises a knowing eyebrow. Clearing his throat, he motions to the petite waitress who stands at the end of the bar with her eyes fixed on our table. "Son, I will leave you to sort your.....complication. I have an early meeting and then I am off to Philadelphia. Check your calendar. I had Nina add a few functions, fundraisers that you and I must attend over the next month. I will see you in a few days." He stands and commands the room, like he always has. Distinguished, handsome, rich and charismatic, my father is the only man I have ever looked up to. Even the youngest women in the room cannot help but sneak a peek at the legendary and solitary Michael Slate.

"Good night, Da." I look down on the page six clipping that Sophie has forwarded me and anger, deep, dark, hot anger pools in my gut. I dial Sophie and it goes straight to her voicemail.

***

Quick and cold, just like that I cut him off. I cannot, will not go back. I will never again be the girl that I once was. I deserve respect. He showed me that. Now he will eat his words. As if he really cares. I suspect that he doesn't. It was all a game to him. Hours become a day and nothing. The days stretch into a week with no sign from him in the slightest. And I know that it is over. A cold ending to something that never really was, now it never will be. Like a common thief, he stole from me, leaving nothing behind but his indelible fingerprints to haunt my memories.

Scotch and water, scotch and water. Sleep. I have developed a taste for the rich man's drink. One night blends into the next. One week becomes two. I pick up a second job to fill my time, cocktail duty for a high end catering outfit. And before I know it, a month has passed and I am comfortably numb. So much so that even the occasional specter of Rhys' scent or touch doesn't burn as it once did. At least, not to my core like it used to. Of course, it is easier to see him alone. He has been conspicuously single in every tabloid rag and paparazzi print. Ever the masochist, I find myself searching for images, a taste, a reminder. Another hit to keep the pain just below the surface, a dull niggle that I can just live with.

His body and his lips are tattooed upon my mind, but my body has almost forgotten. Forgotten how sinfully perfect we fit together. How he could make my blood hum with the slightest brush of his fingers. Almost forgotten, I will keep telling myself that.

Another night, another black tie event. A five thousand dollar per plate dinner and auction for Children's Hospital. The work is tedious at best, but the tips can be ridiculously high. A sea of faceless penguin suits, glittering arm candy and more money than any reasonable person would know what to do with. I work a rich room, and my savings benefit immensely. I line my tray with crystal champagne flutes, and fill each with sparkling, golden Cristal. I have gotten good at the mindless ritual of handing out hundred dollar glasses of champagne to unaffected party goers. Able to glide through a room with casual ease, twelve glasses of bubbly excess propped upon my shoulder, roughly a thousand dollars of champagne per tray. Last weekend, I watched two bored, exquisitely beautiful young women slug down the equivalent of a monthly mortgage in champagne.

"Sophie!" A shrill boom pulls me from my internal reverie. "Hello? Ms. Noelle, are you here?" James, in his too tight, white dinner jacket and pale gray slacks motions for my attention, snapping his pudgy fingers in front of my face. My boss aspires to be polished and professional, but falls short with his flaming cheeks and the shrill rupture of his voice when he gets upset. But he is a shrewd judge of a room, and a domineering brute, for such a short man. "The guests have begun to arrive. Please line up. And whatever is clouding your head, leave it at home, please." He motions to the rest of the cocktail staff to fall in line before his boring speech about how these people are VIPs and we are to treat them as such, no fraternizing or addressing the guests, always keep your tray stocked and be receptive to any special requests. He walks down the line straightening any askew waistcoats, checking for flaws, before he sends us out into the fray. Like a well-oiled machine, we pour slowly into the ballroom in a single-file line and quickly take our cues to go left, right or center, covering every inch of the opulent room, filling every empty hand.

In and out of the kitchen, tray after tray of champagne, I keep their hands and glasses full, never once seeing any of their faces.

"Excuse me, young lady." A silky voice pulls my eyes from the ground. I look upon the chiseled face of an older man, mid-fifties, maybe, very handsome, with kind green eyes. Shining silver curls top his head, faint lines around his eyes betray his obvious penchant for smiling. A slight crooked grin pulls at his full lips. He is familiar, but I know I have never seen him before. I would remember such a glaring example of a distinguished older man. He is polished, refined, yet his eyes are kinder than any others in the room. His eye contact is exact, penetrating but gentle. "Could I bother you for a scotch?" His green eyes twinkle in the dim light of the ballroom, gold flecks picking up the light of the crystal chandeliers that hang above.

"Certainly, sir, how do you like it?" I am captivated by the planes of his face, by his warm eyes.

"Single malt, two fingers, neat. Thank you." He tips his chin to me and turns back to the dapperly suited men who eagerly await the return of his attention. I head to the bar, baffled by the sense of familiarity. I watch intently as Derek, the bartender, pours two fingers of Dalwhinney. The scent coils in my nostrils, twisting my belly in a tight knot. The sweet peat wafts from the glass, bringing a rush of memory sensory overload. I step away from the growing pit of loneliness that has threatened to swallow me for weeks. The pit that I thought I had thoroughly filled and buried. I close my eyes willing the smell to vanish. But as a cruel joke, it grows and twists into a smell so familiar, so laced with vibrant physical memories. Heat simmers in my veins and my stomach twists into a tight knot. I smell him before I see him and my heart sinks.

Chapter 2

Musk and citrus, the smell of being fresh from the beach, I feel his eyes and the heat he is pushing in my direction. I turn and watch him move through the crowd in all his black tie glory. His hair has been closely shorn, his face clean and freshly shaved, he is stalking toward me with an arrogant grin and a humor-filled twinkle in his eyes. His crisp white dinner jacket fits like a glove. What he does to a tuxedo is something to behold. It should be illegal. His broad shoulders and nipped waist were made for a suit. Seeing him like that does a funny thing to me. I can barely hear my own thoughts, or feel my own body. His mere presence and physical perfection roar in my ear. He shines like a perfect gentleman, and I immediately hate him for it. He is so at ease, so sure of himself. Long fingers tug at his black bow tie, loosening it slightly as he steps towards me, the architect of my heartache. Before I can turn and run, he locks me in his sights and holds me hostage.

I have to swallow the urge to bolt from the room. I have to stand and face him. What is he doing here? As he makes his way towards me, I decide that looking busy is my best defense. He wears that damn crooked grin that cuts me to the quick. I step around him and make towards the older gentleman to deliver his scotch. He follows me, a few paces behind, silently. I do not turn back, but I feel him there, the familiar pull of his orbit, the sweet smell of his skin. Damn it! Why is he here? Squeezing between two very eager fundraisers, I make room for the scotch on the small table the men huddle around, hoping that if I bury myself in the crowd, in my work, he will back off.

"Thank you, young lady." With a gut-wrenchingly familiar smile, he picks up the crystal glass and sips the heady liquor, looking over my shoulder with a grin. "Ah, Son, glad you could join us. This is Marcus Phillips." He pulls Rhys to the table, effectively shuffling me out of the way, and I am dumbfounded. "Marcus, this is my son, Rhys. He will be taking over for me someday, and he is far more shrewd than I. You will have to watch out for him." He slaps Rhys on the back as the two men shake hands. I am stuck to the floor, entranced by the whole exchange. "I think we are fine for now, young lady," he prompts, pushing me out of my head and away from the table. I look into his kind eyes as he dismisses me, bewildered. I take the cue and turn so quickly that I almost take out another server with my tray and I stumble over myself trying to get away.

"Actually, I think I would like a drink, Father. Excuse me please, gentlemen." Rhys makes his apologies and follows me silently through the crowd. I speed up, begging for the sanctuary of the kitchen. Pushing through the kitchen doors like they are some sort of a security gate, I let out the breath I have been hoarding only to turn and see Rhys, sauntering through the swinging doors, unaffected by the barrier that is supposed to separate *us* from *them*. When I turn to face him, he shines like a beacon. A beacon of hope that I know offers no real hope at all, a mirage, a lie in the desert that tricks the dying man into drinking sand. I steel myself, square my shoulders and look him in the eye.

"Rhys." My tone is terse, clipped, anything not to jump into his arms, not that he would welcome that anyway.

"Sophie. What are you doing here?" He takes a step forward and I step back.

"Working," I snap, holding my tongue and concentrating on slowing my heart.

"Right, of course," he shakes his head, his long fingers raking across his closely cut hair. Oh, how I miss those curls, wrapped around my fingers. Stop! "I cannot tell you how glad I am to see you." He waits for a reaction, but I offer none. I am reeling on the inside, but outside I am cool as a cucumber. At least I hope that is how it seems. "I am so sorry about what happened. I wanted to explain, but you wouldn't take my calls." He steps closer to me, backing me against a prep table. I have nowhere to go, nowhere to run. I grasp the sides of the table with white knuckles, willing the strength to rise and fill my chest, encase my heart.

"There was nothing to explain. You don't owe me anything, Rhys." The sweetness of his name passing my lips burns.

"Yes, I do, Sophie. I want you to know the truth. I have been going crazy thinking about you. I am sorry." Remorse fills his eyes and his hand reaches out for mine. I pull away from him, knowing I cannot withstand the force of his touch. He will burn me, I can't let him. He puts his hands up in response and backs a step away. "I am sorry that I hurt you. You have every right to be angry."

"I am not angry. That would imply that we had something, which we clearly did not. I am not angry. I am… indifferent." Fury and passion mingle in my blood and my hands tremble as I clench them into tight fists, my fingernails sinking violently into my palm squeezing the reaction back.

"Ms. Noelle! What are you doing? Get back on the floor and circulate." James is stalking towards me with a surefooted purpose until he eyes Rhys. Quickly and seamlessly, he slips into ass kissing mode and shines his dark brown eyes and wolfish grin at Rhys. "Ah, Mr. Slate, I am James, it is lovely to meet you. I hope that Sophie is not bothering you." He turns his eyes on me, all traces of civility gone. "Sophie, is there a problem here?"

"Um."

"No, James. Thank you. There is no problem. I would just like a moment to speak with Sophie here, would that be alright?" Rhys' commanding, charming demeanor diffuses James almost immediately, at least on the surface. His eyes are full of disapproval as he looks me up and down, I can read his expression. It reads *No fraternizing with the guests!* He tugs at the bottom of his dinner jacket, brushing phantom lint off his lapel. He does not fill a suit the way Rhys does, his stubby arms and wide neck are almost too much for his cuffs and tie to contain. And the buttons on his jacket are clearly working overtime, holding in a little pot belly. His pale skin is flushed and splotchy, exasperation betraying him.

"Of course, Mr. Slate." The way he changes from ass kisser to ass kicker is fluid and unnerving. "Sophie, you may take your break." And he dismisses me with a curt wave. "Please, Mr. Slate, if there is anything I can do for you this evening, do not hesitate to ask." He pushes through the swinging doors, into the ballroom. Rhys wraps his strong fingers around my elbow and leads me out of the kitchen, across to the far corner of the ballroom and outside to the stone patio.

"What are you doing here, Rhys?"

"My father and I are generous benefactors to the Children's Hospital. Why wouldn't you take my calls?" Swinging me around to face him, his steely resolve has dissipated into an unsure panic. His eyes are urgent, begging for an explanation. Why does he care?

"I changed phones, changed numbers. I never got a call." Now I am just cutting him to cut.
A heavy sigh heaves in his chest, deep and full.

"Sophie! I have been going out of my mind."

"It has been three weeks, Rhys, why do you care so much? Why does any of it even matter to you?" Anger blooms in my chest, replacing the uneasy sorrow that I was so afraid of. I stand with my back straight, feet firmly planted in reality. He may be bigger than me, but I am bigger than this. His grip tightens around my arms and he shakes me slightly, anger angling to replace whatever it was that he was feeling as well.

"Why do I care?" Fury sparks in his dark green eyes, as his fingers dig into my flesh. "I care about you!" He releases me in a rush and I fall back on my heels. "I care about you, Sophie. I did not want to hurt you."

"But you did!" I snap back before I can run it through my filter. He steps into my space and cups the back of my head. Oh, the exquisite feel of his hands in my hair, his strength holding me close. I have to fight the urge to curl into his grasp, the pull to wrap myself in his arms. He steadies me, his finger pressing beneath my chin, tilting my head. Our eyes meet and the pain reflected in his face is almost too much to bear. Why am I crumbling so easily? Where are those defenses I have been working on? They are scattered across the stone patio, blowing in the breeze fifteen stories above the city.

"I didn't mean to," he whispers. "Please give me a chance to explain." He is pleading. Looking into his eyes, I cannot lie, or pretend. The truth hurts, looking at him in his perfect tuxedo, while I am in a cocktail waitress uniform makes the truth that much more painful. Words rush from my mouth, a flurry of insecure thoughts and misguided judgments, a stream of consciousness that has been nagging me from the start.

"Nadja is a fucking model. Your friends are Ivy League educated. I am serving drinks. One of these things is not like the others." I step back, out of his grasp, out of the cloud of confusion and longing that he creates with just a touch. "We don't belong together. I do not belong. It was never going to work between us. Seeing that picture of you and Nadja just reminded me of the truth." I stare at the grain in the stones beneath my feet, pushing back the deluge of trapped emotions. Feelings I have been pushing back and drinking down since I first realized how stupid I was to believe we could be anything other than a torrid weekend romp. "This was never going to end well for me. You need a woman to challenge you, not fall flat on her back. You would tire of me quickly." His arms circle me and pull me into his chest before I can protest, and I am grateful. The charge between us is stronger than I remember and my head presses into his chest without a thought. My body has surrendered so easily. But my mind…my mind is reeling and ready for a fight.

"You don't challenge me? That is all you have done from the moment I set eyes on you. Believe me, I could find a woman to follow me around and warm my bed. That is not what this is. You have character and strength. You are genuine and good hearted. You could easily be on the arm of any one of these men. But I will tell you now, if you were on anyone else's arm, I would not, could not accept it. I would hate it, a white hot, blinding hate. Just thinking about you with someone else makes me seethe with jealousy. I am sorry I did that to you." His heart flutters into that familiar, steady rhythm and my mind zeroes in on it. He tips my head to the heavens and bites his lip before kissing me lightly at the corner of my scowl. My lips flutter and turn, unable to resist him. He pulls me into a deep, needy kiss, our tongues tangle, stroking one another. A deep sigh escapes my chest and he becomes more heated, his hands twisting in my hair. Just as I am about to completely lose my breath, we are torn from each other by the shattering of pottery. James is standing on the threshold of the patio, a large pot that held a ficus behind the French doors, scattered about the stone. The doors flung open in his fervor to stop the fraternization, no doubt.

"Ms. Noelle!" he roars, stomping towards me. Now his buttons really do look as if they are about to burst. His barrel chest is puffed and his face is stern. Rhys pulls me into his chest, a protective reaction to James' aggressive approach. "This is unacceptable, Ms. Noelle. I am so sorry, Mr. Slate. Ms. Noelle will be dealt with, I assure you." He goes to grab my arm and Rhys reacts so quickly my head spins. He swings me behind his back and squares his shoulders to James. Rhys' lean frame looms high above the stocky, middle-aged build of James.

"There will be no need to deal with Ms. Noelle." Rhys leans into James.

"I am sorry, Mr. Slate, but we have a strict policy against fraternization and Ms. Noelle has clearly violated that policy." He puffs his chest at Rhys, trying to match his power, but he cannot.

"That is perfectly fine, James, because Ms. Noelle quits."

"What? Wait, no I don't!" I step around Rhys. "Rhys, what are you doing?" I slap his hand away and step away from him. "James, I am sorry, please. I don't quit."

"Yes, you do!" Rhys declares, his stern face a clear indication of his determination. He turns back to James. "She quits. Come along, Ms. Noelle." His tongue curls around my name like a snake, strangling its prey. He tugs my hand and pulls me into the ballroom, knowing that the scene from outside will not follow us in. I rip my hand from his and turn to him in a fit of rage, ready to unleash the fury of this woman, when his father steps up behind him.

"There you are, Son. They are getting ready to seat everyone for dinner and the auction." He looks from Rhys' face to mine and smiles. Stepping between us, he takes my hand. Watching my eyes, he slowly raises my hand to his mouth, planting a gentle kiss before revealing a slightly crooked grin that melts my heart. "I am Michael Slate. And you are?" He doesn't release my hand, running his fingers along the ridge of my knuckles, he waits, eyebrows raised.

"I am Sophie. It's lovely to meet you, Mr. Slate." His lips curl into a knowing smile and he places my hand back at my side.

"Ah…Sophie, of course. It is lovely to finally meet you. I have heard a lot about you. Please, let us dispense with the stuffy formalities." He leans in close and whispers in an amused tone, "You can call me Michael." His eyes glimmer with humor as he looks from me to Rhys. "Son, I think I can handle these vultures." His clever dismissal frees Rhys' conscience and he smiles. They share the same disarming crooked grin, the same kind green eyes, and the same twisted sense of gallantry. "I hope we meet again, Ms. Noelle," he calls after us, as Rhys practically drags me across the ballroom and out into the hall.

I tear my hand from his and back against the wall opposite him, preparing for a showdown. I cannot believe that he just quit my job, humiliated me in front of his father, and then dragged me out of the room like a petulant child.

"Was this a coincidence or a plot?" I demand. His smile is mocking, amused by my obvious anger, and my inability to manage it.

"A bit of both, a happy accident, maybe fate." His grin is electric, like a child on Christmas morning. "I have been biding my time, waiting for the right moment. I figured you needed time to cool down. Yes, we are here because I knew I would be close to you. I was planning, however, to see you after the weekend, after I had settled on a plan of action. I had no idea you would be here, tonight. How could I?" He takes a step closer and I step back. "You caught me by surprise, a very happy surprise."

"Why?" My voice is smaller than I had intended. He takes a step closer and I step back. He sighs in resignation.

"I told you the last time we were together that I was finding it harder and harder to be away from you. Leaving was so hard, staying away has been even harder. I just want to be near you." His confession, open and honest, tugs at my bereft heart. My heart takes off, throbbing in the empty space he left.

"I was not looking for anything when you stumbled on me that night, Sophie. I did not plan on you. You were a complete surprise. The most perfect, delicious, sexy surprise. You caught me off guard. The moment I saw you I knew I had to have you. I have never felt that way before. I am unaccustomed to being taken in like that. I didn't like it. But, you, you climbed inside me and made yourself at home. You live here now." He touches his long finger to his temple. "And here." He splays his hand across his heart and squeezes, flexing his fingers, digging into his own, perfect flesh.

He steps closer and I stay still. A slight smile rises at the corner of his mouth, he reads me like a book. He doesn't reach out to touch me, just stands closer, taking a deep breath.

"I couldn't get a hold of you. You cancelled your phone." Bewildered eyes stare back at me as his voice cracks, almost imperceptibly. "Your column went silent. You can be quite the ghost when you want to be. I have never been cut off like that." He takes a step closer and I have to fight the very real urge to launch myself into his waiting arms. I want him to hold me, to touch me with those hands. But I have had too much time to think about it, too much time to stew. I need more from him, more information. I need my pound of flesh. I look up into his eyes and see the growing confidence, believing he has won. "I couldn't have you thinking so badly of me."

"You don't care what people think of you," I declare, trying desperately to hold on to my slipping resolve.

"I don't," he says, his hands lightly brush my arms, before he rests them on my shoulders gingerly, testing the waters, teasing every skin cell, calling my blood to rush to his touch. His silky palms slide up the pebbled skin of my arms before returning to my shoulders. His thumb dips into the hollow of my throat and he has gone too far. "I care what *you* think."

Before my mind can even hear what he has said, my mouth launches into the tirade I have been holding for weeks.

"Why did you come here? That night with Collin, why did you come? You could have just flown straight through. No *layover*. It would all have faded, like it should have." That is not the truth, but I am wounded, needing to strike at him. Wanting him to feel the pain that I felt, if anything he says is true. He winces at the venom I spew and steps back, his eyes turning dark. He scowls at me for a moment, an angry bull nursing a superficial wound.

"Are you trying to be hurtful?" His voice is low and serious. His smoky eyes scorch me with a raw intensity I have never witnessed. "Are you *so* angry at me?" I take a step closer, regretting pushing him away. He frowns, knitting his brows together and I take a deep breath, knowing I will only have one chance to get all the words out.

"No. Yes. I don't know! I just feel like I can't trust you, and I know I cannot trust myself around you. I have been two steps behind since the first night we met. Nadja was always there in Miami. And then you are there with her in the paper. Fine, but why? Why did you keep coming on to me after that? Just to hurt me? I don't understand undertaking such extreme efforts for a piece on the side."

"You are very insecure," he declares, too assured of himself and his opinion of me.

"You don't know me."

"I know parts of you very well." He leers at me and curls his lip, leaning in closer.

"You are lewd, Mr. Slate."

"You bring out the best in me, Sophie, what can I say?" He takes a step closer and I back away, the dance becoming too much. "You are trying to wound me, Sophie, but I see now that it is because I wounded you first."

"How could I wound you? You hold all the heavy weapons in this fight."

"Are we fighting?" The pause is chilling. "You don't want to fight with me, Sophie. You will not win." His rapid shift in mood clears the air. Devoid of all his playfulness, he is cold, serious and out for blood.

"I have nothing to fight with." My voice is small, but the weight and truth of the words is heavy and disheartening. He comes and goes as he pleases. Jet set and unencumbered, the world laid out at his feet, most women hovering there as well. How can I compete with that?

"You have this." He reaches out, gently grazing my lips with his thumb. He rests his palm, heavy against my chest, leaning into me. Lowering his head, he takes a deep, controlled hit from my neck. He runs his nose up the curve under my chin and I swear I hear my teeth rattle. "And this," he murmurs against my neck, flexing his hand over my heart, while his tongue dips into the hollow at the base of my throat. It works. He ignites my blood in a heartbeat and slowly lets the anger seep out under the safe conduct of his gentle breath sliding across my skin. How easily he confounds me, proof of his utter control. I know I am no match for him. His gentle, dangerous brand of dominance my newest and most favorite weakness. His hands slide down my arms, sending a delicious chill racing down my spine. He laces his fingers with mine, so sensual and safe, pulling them to his mouth. Kissing the back of both of my hands, he sets my skin on fire.

"Do you know how much it hurts to be right here, in front of you and not be able to hold you? You have plenty of weaponry. Come," he coaxes, pulling me down the hall to the bank of elevators. "Let's finish this conversation," his smile gives him away, "in *private*."

When we get to his room, he pours me a drink and proffers me to sit, before he launches into his explanation.

"I was committed to Nadja and the gala long before we met. We co-founded that foundation with my mother almost ten years ago. I honor my commitments, Sophie. Yes, we were together, as we have been every year. It is just part of the game." There is that word again, *game*. My eyes narrow on him as he takes a seat at the other end of the sofa. "The press line, the pictures. It all brings in more money. The gossip columnists can write whatever they like, as long as we keep raising millions." His tone is almost reproachful, making me feel suddenly selfish for focusing on something so trivial. "Nadja is a model, as you pointed out. The press line, red carpets, photographers, it's her drug, her natural state of being. It is one of the few things she actually brings to the charity, all of her publicity and preening catches people's attention." He slides closer to me on the couch, still looking so crisp and completely unruffled in his custom tuxedo. He pulls on the bow tie to loosen the grip on his throat and I gasp. I want to undo that tie. He eyes me with a knowing grin before dropping his fingers from the tie.

"I didn't sleep with her if that's what you think. In fact, I was so distracted by thoughts of you that I forgot an entire portion of my speech. I wore a gardenia in my lapel so I could smell you all night. And, if I remember correctly…" His fingers brush the back of my hand. "We had a very enlightening exchange that very evening, do you remember?" He bites his lip and closes his eyes for a long moment, humming at the delight of his memory. I squirm, remembering all too well what we did, flashes of his silky voice guiding my hands blaze a trail in my head. It's as if he has planted a fresh memory, as if I could feel it all again right now. Amusement lights his eyes as they open to the sight of me trying not to writhe and squeal at his provocation. "That is what drove me to come see you. That is why I showed up when I did. And thank God that I did because what could have happened if I didn't?" Inching ever closer, he reaches out and squeezes my knee.

"How much more time are we going to waste?" His heat floods through me in a torrent, all the old sensations and sparks alight between us and my body hums for his brand, his hands, his mouth. And my heart is sated, rolling around in the warm delight of his adamant declaration. Winding his hand around my neck, he brushes his thumb across my cheek and looks at my lips. This is the moment, the moment that I cave or stand.

"Oh, no." I hop to my feet before he can pin me to the couch, away from his hypnotic hands. He glowers for a split second before his eyes glaze over with a licentious, manipulative intent. Every inch of my body springs to attention with his smoking look. I tamp it down, unwilling to let my body betray me. I will not stay. He rises with purpose from the couch, slow and lithe. His eyes are narrowed on me and he pulls that lip through his teeth. A rattle erupts in my loins in unison with his teeth, ringing in my blood. Fight it! "That is not going to work." I put my hands up in defense.

"Are you saying *no*?" he scoffs, unbelieving and moves ever closer.

"Yes, I believe I am." I meet his stare with little capacity to return his intensity.

"No." He takes a step closer, rolling the word over his tongue. "Nobody says no."

"I do." The resolve is leaking from my toes, pulling me into a quicksand of longing and weak knees. I need to get out now if I'm going to make it at all.

"Hmm….twice now," he murmurs quietly, scratching at his freshly shaved skin, pulled taught along his sculpted jaw. "Do you want me to beg?" His eyebrows crease and his lips curl into a sour scowl.

"A little begging might be good for your ego."

"I have never had to beg for anything."

"Well, Mr. Slate, there is a first time for everything. And if you really want something, you should be willing to do whatever it takes to get it. And if that means to beg, then you will beg." I bite back a wide, face-cracking grin. God, this is fun, but I better get out before I lose the upper hand. I make my way towards the door. "I think we solved a mystery here tonight." His quizzical eyes search my face. "*How to keep Rhys' attention*," I muse, teasing him. "Just say, *NO*."

The humor doesn't touch him. He looms over me, even though he is steps away.

"What is happening here?"

"I am going home."

"Why?"

"There is something more. Something you're holding back. I don't want any part of it."

"Sophie, you have my attention. Please." He reaches for me, hooking his finger around my thumb, trying to pull me nearer.

"I am glad to have your attention, Rhys. Now you can watch me leave." My hand is on the door and he is at my back.

"Wait. That's it?" Shaking his head in disbelief, I revel in my tiny victory, straighten my back and smile sweetly.

"That's it." Pulling the door open, he lets me step into the hall, leaning on the door jam. He pulls my hand, not allowing me to get any further away. God, if I had known that playing hard to get was so fun, I would have done it sooner.

"When can I see you?" His thumb caresses the back of my hand.

"When you are ready," I say, stepping into the elevator, taking my hand from his.

"Ready for what?" he quizzes before the doors slide closed.

"Ready to tell me the truth. The whole truth." All I have is a disingenuous smile as the doors separate us. I am glad for the solitude, but ache for his presence. I got out of there just in time. I don't know how much resolve I had left. The thirty minute drive will surely slow my racing pulse and calm my frayed nerves.

Chapter 3

Driving home, adrenaline courses through me like a raging river. I am agitated, exhilarated and turned on. My skin prickles with heat. A slow simmer builds in my belly, the lazy after effects of Rhys' mere presence. It is hot and still, the dark skies clear of clouds. Humidity hangs in the air from the summer rains. The bright white moon follows me home. Tugging my skirt up my thighs, tiny lightning strikes flare beneath my flesh where my fingers brush against my sensitive skin. I do it again and the sensation rings in my ears. Again on the other leg, the pads of my fingers like a velvet whisper across my hot flesh. Goose bumps pebble my exposed white thigh, and I am practically panting. Shifting in my seat, a silky wetness spreads between my legs. The heat and wet is an exquisite tease. I am so hot, and equally bothered.

Deep down I had harbored hope that he would show up and gallantly sweep me off my feet. But now that he is here I am not sure what to do. I had longed for him to show, but didn't count on it. Now he finds me flustered and caught off guard. I speed up, needing to get home quickly, to peel myself from this uniform that I no longer need, to slip into a bath and wash it all away. My pulse spikes as my foot presses the gas. I am propelled by my own singing blood. My whole body aches, aches to be caressed, kissed. Damn it! A breath catches in my throat as I turn into my neighborhood. My racing pulse pounds in each of my limbs, the longing has reached a fever pitch and I cannot wait to get inside.

A ravenous need is threatening to consume me and it must be tamed. I will tame it myself.

I run a steaming hot bath and strip quickly, impatient and irritated at what he so easily does to me. Slipping beneath the steamy, soap filled water, I try and relax. Dropping my shoulders, I sink into the water and close my eyes. But damn him, he is right there. Behind my lids he dances, that crooked grin and tight body taunting me. A growl escapes my throat and I startle myself. I let the warm water loosen my muscles and soften my skin before my hands begin to travel. Up and over the soft curve of my breasts, I take a deep breath, waiting to feel the fire I have so sorely missed. My hands mimic his, following the trails he blazed across my skin. I cup myself and pinch my aching nipples, twisting them between my fingers. My fingers skate up my neck and across my collar bone as a small whimper escapes my lips. Yes, this is what I so desperately need. It is dangerous to be around him, to even lay eyes on him when I am so tightly wound. I should do this every day just as a precaution. Surely, I can supply myself with the pleasure I need. The pleasure that will keep me firmly grounded in reality.

My fingers circle my belly button, float over my hips and beneath the water. I try and steady my breath, to focus on my hands, my burning core and the heat that is erupting from between my thighs. Even under the water I can feel the heat, the need that churns within. Teasing myself, I gently run the tip of my finger up and over my begging mound. Through the tightly shorn curls, I twist and tease, hoping for relief, hoping to ignite that lovely burn. Dipping my finger just between my lips, I seek out the treasure. That tightly wound bundle of nerves that can release me from this hell, this torturous aching. Around and around, my fingers roll and press. My breath quickens and my core tightens. Yes, relief is close at hand. Around and around until my head begins to spin, a dull hum settling all over my skin.

"Just a little more," I moan out loud in anticipation, and rub harder. Deeper, I push two fingers beyond the folds and sink into myself. "Aahh." Yes. The sensation builds, higher and higher until I am at the cliff. Standing on the edge, just a little more. I press harder, rub faster. Yet I remain perched, stuck. I rub and rub and rub until my fingers twitch, until my body protests. Nothing! A whimper rips from my lips as I push harder, rub faster and press down on my clit until my fingers are pushed off.

My body has betrayed me! A frustrated roar erupts from my chest as my hands fall to my sides. Damn it! I am stuck and more frustrated than ever. I move to try again, but my over worked core cries out in denial. And I have lost the battle. I am doomed to remain on this edge. Looking out over the abyss that I want so badly to swallow me up, I am doomed and anchored to the spot. Unable to relieve myself, I curse Rhys and angrily climb from the tub.

After a brutal scrubbing with a towel, I lotion my skin head to toe, throw on cotton shorts and a tank and make my way to the kitchen. If I cannot relieve this frustration the old fashioned way, perhaps I can push it away with food. I search my sadly empty cupboards and fridge, nothing. I guess I will have to settle for yet another peanut butter and jelly sandwich. If I do not go shopping and buy some groceries soon, I am sure to turn into a human PB & J sandwich. I pull the strawberry preserves from the fridge and grab the bread. Searching for an almost empty jar of peanut butter, I hear a faint knock on my door that sends my pulse racing. I look at the clock on the stove and it is after midnight.

"Sophie? Are you up?" I freeze, my muscles twisting tighter. I didn't think I could be wound any tighter, but I was wrong. Just the sound of his voice twists me up in knots so tight I could snap right where I stand. I wait for a moment to make sure I actually heard his voice, and decide what to do. Should I pretend to be asleep? Wait for him to leave? Even as I think it, I know I don't want that. He has frayed my nerves, twisted my body up, but in the most delicious way and I know I do not want to pass up this opportunity. I do not want him to turn and walk away. I wait, wanting to make him wait.

Standing against the counter, I try and catch my breath, to tame my heartbeat before I answer the door, but I am robbed. Robbed of the opportunity to let him in as I hear a key slide into the lock, and my teeth start grinding, my jaw so tense it may shatter.

"Sophie?" His voice is softer as he slowly pushes the door open and peeks around. Standing stock still, I wait. He pulls his key from the door, closing it quietly behind him before he turns. His eyes grow wide when he finally sees me, hopefully appearing casual as I hold on to the counter for fear that I may just haul off and hit him.

A wide, guilty smile spreads across his face when our eyes meet. A slight tick at the corner of his eye tells me he sees the rage flaring in mine. Before I can burst into flames, he closes the door behind him and drops his keys to *my* house onto the kitchen table.

"I'm ready." I regard him shrewdly, feeling anxious and thrilled. "I will tell you anything you want to know, Sophie. All you have to do is ask." I turn my back unable yet to form a response, and pull out two more pieces of bread and spread them with peanut butter.

He presses up behind me, wrapping his arms around me and I freeze. Summoning every ounce of resistance I can, but he pushes me over the edge with a swift kiss on my shoulder and I jump. Pushing him across the narrow expanse of the kitchen, I press him to the refrigerator and hand him a sandwich.

"You stay there, no touching." Excitement flares in his eyes like a slowly stoking fire. He is too sure of himself and it is maddening and electrifying. I want to let him do all sorts of depraved things to me. But I cannot just fall down for him. I don't want this to be easy. But, what I wouldn't do to have those lips on my needy skin. The corner of his mouth turns in that crooked way that makes my insides beg for mercy. Oh, I hate that he can read me like that! I have to make him wait, I can do that much. Make him sweat it out, suffer at least a little bit, if even for a moment. I hop up onto the counter and sit across from him, my feet swinging high above the kitchen floor. He watches me take a bite of my peanut butter sandwich before stepping closer. I press my foot to the center of his chest and hold him at bay with my leg stretched across the kitchen. "Uh uh." The peanut butter is stuck to the roof of my mouth.

"What was that, Ms. Noelle? I cannot understand you. Did you say come here?" He slides his fingers around my ankle, but I push him back, shaking my head. I hold a finger up, needing a minute, a time out to take a drink of milk and release my jaw from this peanut butter prison. I quickly wash my sandwich down while his face flares with humor. "You want me to stay over here? Really?"

"Yes. You cannot just come over here, *let yourself in*, and rub up on me like nothing happened. You do not have that right, Mr. Slate." A silly grin hinders my delivery.

"Then I will earn that right," he returns, his face serious and determined. He has caught me off guard and I have no response, and before I can try to form one, he takes over. "I am serious, Sophie." He stays glued to the fridge. "I am sorry that I hurt you. I will *never* do it again." The conviction in his eyes is heavy and honest, filling the silence between us. I drop my foot and end the standoff, unable to deny him when he has declared his intentions so boldly. We both slowly finish our peanut butter and jelly, allowing the silence to settle between us.

"Tell me about her."

"There is a long history between us. Our fathers were business partners at one point, our mothers close friends." He looks at me through clear eyes. "We grew up together, we grew bored together." He pauses, shaking his head. "When you have the world at your fingertips and you are still bored, things can go very wrong. She was like a force of nature. She would breeze in and out of town between jobs, or we would meet on holiday. We all traveled in the same circles, when you went certain places, you just knew you would run into someone. But, out of the blue, she ran off and married some photographer two years ago." There is no emotion in his eyes, he is just relaying a story that happened to someone else. "They promptly divorced seven months later, and she came running back, as was her way." He looks up at me through dark lashes, but I offer no reaction. I want to hear it all, so I bite my tongue and listen. "Things escalated quickly, as they always do with her, but this time was different. Watching Matthew and Olivia plan for their wedding, and looking at myself. Myself and Nadja, it just made me sick. I didn't want to be that guy anymore. Taking things just because you can, using people because they let you."

I am frozen, listening to him spill a lifetime of dirt in my kitchen, while clutching a peanut butter and jelly sandwich that I made.

"I didn't want any of it any more. There was no challenge. I grew up, gave in and started working with my father in New York and I have kept myself sufficiently busy ever since." He pops the last piece of sandwich in his mouth before washing it down with a swig of milk. My mind races in the silent moment. Wanting to know so much more, but so grateful that he has so easily opened up, I let the notion wash over me and decide that it is enough. For now, it is enough.

"Her father, Viktor Vladova, his company is being liquidated. I have been working with him to try and salvage what we can, and that is where Nadja comes in. She showed up in New York that first day that I met you, come to think of it. She showed up begging me to help her father. I told her then that we were over, but I would do what I could for Victor. I had to remind her again, in Miami, and she has been a pain in my side ever since."

I wrinkle my nose and try to look playful. Not to let him see any of this information bog me down. I can be comfortable with his past, if that is what it is. We are adults. We are bound to have lived before we knew one another, there is no fault there, just a little occasional haunting from a supermodel. He takes a step closer and holds his hands out.

"Can I touch you now?" I cannot even play coy, and I don't try. I want him to touch me, my skin is silently begging for the warm brand of his hand. I put my legs down and slide to the edge of the counter, eager.

"If you must." I wiggle my shoulders as he places those hands on my hips. They sear my skin with a white hot lust that oozes from his strong fingertips. He pulls me close to him and I wrap my feet around his hips. In a flash, his hands are in my hair, pushing it back, fisting it and tugging before our mouths tangle in a languid, passion filled kiss. My lips swell from the force of his mouth as he moves to my neck and across my shoulder.

"God, I have missed this," he murmurs between kisses. Before I can mutter a word, he has my mouth in a tangle again, his tongue pushing against mine in a sinful dance. I moan out loud and it sets him off. He rips the shirt over my head, wrapping his hands around my breasts faster than they can fall. He dips his head and takes one into his mouth, laving the delicate skin around my nipple with the flat of his tongue before he sucks the bud into his mouth and nips me with his teeth. My passion spikes and I grip his head in my hands and tug him away. He looks up at me with feral, lusty eyes and all my defenses are spent. I cannot believe that I lasted this long because I am about to pounce on this man.

"Take me to bed," I demand in a throaty whisper that I have never heard before.

Chapter 4

"My pleasure." So easily he picks me up and walks down the hall to my bedroom, my legs locked around his trim waist. I pull the shirt from his head and he drops me to the bed as I toss it over his shoulder. In one quick movement, he whips my little shorts off and drops his pants. Well, we made quick work of that. He drops his fists to the bed and crawls over me as I back away from him moving up the bed. His nimble body twists and turns like a kinetic sculpture, fluid lines and elegant movement.

I run my fingers along his jaw. The skin is smooth and tight and I must have frowned because he immediately offers an explanation.

"I thought clean face…clean *Slate*?" He waits and I smile up at him. "You don't like it?" he questions. And I realize that I do like it, and the idea of a clean slate. I will take him any way I can get him. Clean slate, shrouded in shadow. Either way, this is right where I want to be.

"I like the sound of that."

"Stay still and let me look at you. Fuck, you are so sexy," he declares with utter conviction. I tip my head to the ceiling, letting my eyes drift shut listening to his reverie. I miss this place, the space we inhabit together. It's like a different plane, a different world. His hands circle the delicate skin at my inner thighs, making me hot and eager. "Open your eyes. I want you to see what you have done. What you do to me." Peeking up at him, I behold the most glorious sight. His strong, long fingers fisted around his long, thick shaft. His hand gliding slowly up and down, his silky skin pulling so tight it looks ready to rip. He hisses through his teeth, "Look what you've done, Beautiful." I'm mesmerized by his hand, by his glistening cock. "I need you so bad, I'm rock hard, so hard it almost hurts." A hiss escapes his mouth before he pulls his lips into his mouth and groans. There is a shining god between my legs, all defenses spent, I surrender.

"You make me crazy so easily, Sophie. Watch," he implores, taking my hand into his. Now we both feel the stroke of his velvety skin wrapped around steel, and it is enough to make me shudder in delight. "Watch me come apart for you," he whispers, pressing his thumb to the tiny bundle of nerves at the top of my sex. It sends a charge straight through me. My toes curl and an effusion of angelic white noise fills my head as he sinks slowly into my begging, pulsing body. Teeth gritted, grasping for the control he so desperately clings to, he slides out then pushes his way back in. Each time, he pushes deeper, slower. "Ah, Sophie." He pulls my knee, hitching it up over his hip to get the angle he needs to bury himself in my depths, pressing slowly, allowing me to stretch around him.

One last gentle thrust and the fullness threatens my sanity. He feels so good. Every cell hums and twists around him. I struggle to keep my eyes on him as he stills, buried deep inside me. His emerald eyes ablaze, hooded lids and all. We are one, connected, throbbing for one another, trapped in each other's stare. The ghost of a crooked grin crosses his lips and his eyes fall shut as his head rolls back.

"This is where I belong." A litany, professed to the heavens. "Please, Sophie, I need this. I need you."

"You have me," the strangled words escape my dry throat while my body pulses around him, begging for movement. His long, lean body looms high above me, still. When his eyes open they are fierce and hungry, like a jungle cat. He drops over me, fists buried in the mattress on either side of me, and demands I hold on to something. My leaden arms reach behind and feel around for the iron scroll of the headboard. Pressing his forehead to mine, every atom in the room directs its energy to that one point. Our cells mingle and dance a ferocious tango.

"I didn't know I could miss someone so much. Hmmm...you're killing me, Sophie. And I love it."

My heart skips to the casual use of such an off limits word for him. He is buried between my legs, his hard, planed chest pressed against mine. Yet, the most intense electricity radiates from the single point where his head rests against mine. Connected in every way, tied to each other by a force we cannot see. He starts to move, rocking slowly into me, swaying his hips from side to side. One final deliciously slow slide and he pulls back. The glimmer in his eye tells me to hold on tight and he slams into me, crushing himself against me. His balls slap against me as he plunges deeper. His pelvis rubs at my clit with every powerful thrust. Every inch of my body is on fire. From my toes to the top of my head, I cannot make out a single sensation, but Rhys. He is everything, everywhere. I tighten my grip on the iron as the thrusts become more needy and frantic.

"Come with me, Sophie!" he roars and we crumble together. My loins milk him, pulling him deeper, missing the familiar heat as he loses himself deep inside. I feel each white hot stream filling me beyond capacity as he groans, burying his face in my neck. We float back down to earth together, still connected, still writhing against each other. His full weight rests on me, pressing me into the mattress and I am on cloud nine. I have missed the weight of a man, the weight of *this* man. We lie sated, still as one for a long moment before he pulls out and I wince at the loss of his heat. He pulls me to his chest and I focus on his heartbeat.

"I'm sorry…" A whisper, buried deep in my hair.

"Sorry for what?" Unable to keep the purr from my voice, I nuzzle into his neck and take a deep hit of my drug of choice.

"I thought this would be easy. Something light, just a bit of fun, that we could both emerge unscathed. With maybe a few memories, but not much more, I was so wrong. I see now that is not an option for us." He has me wrapped in his arms, my head tucked under his chin. I cannot see his face, cannot fathom where this is heading. Panic trickles into my chest, a fist clutching at my still racing heart, strangling my heated pulse. Could he cut me off just seconds after pulling out? My eyes dart about the room, seeking a point to focus on.

Something to look at, anywhere, but to his strong arms wrapped comfortably around me. I am suddenly glad that I cannot see his face because he, too, cannot see mine, cannot see the emotion that threatens to tear me down. My mind is racing, grasping and scraping for an excuse, an out. Paranoia racks my body as I scramble for an upper hand before he can crush me with a dismissal. The faintest wiggle of a tear threatens to expose me. I am raw, open and flayed by what we have just done. And now I am to be broken.

"I have to have you, Sophie, all the time." He pulls me closer, cradling me against his chest. Relief fills my lungs and I take a deep breath of his musk, elated that my paranoia is so easily discounted and shocked by my ability to get so negative. "I'm hooked. I don't think I can leave you again. It's too hard to bear. I want you with me." He nuzzles my neck before pushing me back so we can look each other in the eye, and he has caught me completely off guard. "Come back to New York with me."

Oh, the offer is too good. Run away with this sexual demigod, lock ourselves away in some glamorous, art Deco high rise, lose myself in the city. Before I can talk myself out of it, I know I want to go.

"I could take a few days off. I have never been to New York." I mull over the articles I have promised Mary, and I'm sure I can manage them from New York. And, thanks to Rhys, I no longer have to worry about my second job. My heart begins to swell at the thought of being in New

York, at the thought of being with him in New York.

"Not a few days," he shakes his head, staring at the ceiling, "more like….I don't know. Just come. Come to New York. I want to see you every day. I want to hold you every night. I need to touch you and smell you and taste you." Oh my, his words wash over me, and I almost lose my head. I want to give him all those things. "Indefinitely," he declares, his eyes trapping me in a death grip. And there it is. The catch.

"What? Rhys, you know I cannot do that. I have a life, here."

"I want you in *my* life."

"I will be in your life, if you put me there." He hesitates for a moment.
"My everyday life."

"Rhys, I have my own life here. I have a job and my grandmother. I cannot just leave."

"But, I can take care of you, you wouldn't have to worry about anything."

"Rhys! I don't want that. I don't want you to take care of me. My life is mine, it is real and it is dull and it is mine. If you really want me in your life, then make room for me and everything about me, but I will not rely on you. I won't become some accessory, hanging on for dear life, waiting for you to come home, begging for your attention. You wouldn't want me then, and I don't want that."

"I want to give you the world, Sophie."

"I already have my own world, Rhys, but I want you to be a part of it. We can be a part of each others' worlds. Please, I do not want to fight."

"Alright, I am a smart man, I know when I have been beaten, temporarily." Narrowing his eyes at me, he grins. "But I want to be closer to you, and commandeering a jet every time I need to see you is not fiscally responsible."

"Am I not a good investment?" Teasing, I run my fingers over his chest and feel a tremor run through him.

"More of a gamble," he laughs and the throaty sound is beautiful. "But, good lord, Beautiful, you have already paid out in spades. I don't usually gamble, but I do know that you don't step away from the table when you are winning. I will figure something out."

"Don't you have to work?" I am concerned, knowing how important his father's company and his own foundations are to him.

"I do." He kisses my forehead. "I always do. But, I am always working." He taps his temple with a slight grin on his lips. "Work smarter," he quips. His hands run up and down my back, lulling me into a trance. "All joking aside, there is a big development deal that Matthew and I have been working on, I will take the week to wrap it up. We will revisit on Friday." He cups my backside and kneads my fleshy tail, distracting me from what he just said. "How's that?"

"Hmm?" My eyes are heavy, my limbs tired and limp.

"Were you even listening to me, Ms. Noelle?"

"Yes, I'm sorry. Revisit on Friday. That sounds perfect." An unwelcome yawn erupts from my chest and I can't fight sleep. Rhys reaches around behind him, tugging the chain on my bedside lamp. "Will you stay the weekend with me?" I ask in the dark.

"I thought you would never ask, Beautiful. Sleep now, Sophie." He kisses the top of my head as I nuzzle into the hollow of his throat, taking a deep breath of his smell. This place is sure to give me wonderful dreams, and for the first time in weeks, I fall asleep without the ache.

I am startled awake by the ringing of my phone. "Hello!" A little too gruff, a little too tired. The sun is already high in the sky and I am sure I have slept away half of the morning. I roll over to find Rhys gone.

"Sophie! Are you coming in today or what?"

"Oh, Mary, I am sorry, I forgot!"

"Well, I am here. I have already done the layout, so I will have to show you that another time." It takes me a moment to collect my thoughts and wake up. Shit, I was supposed to go into the paper today. Where is Rhys?

"Listen, Mary. I am not going to make it in today. Um…Rhys is here."

"Mr. Money bags showed up, huh? Were you expecting him? I thought you two weren't talking."

"We weren't. But, you know. We ran into each other last night, and.."

"Oh, I see how it is. He breezes into town with his deep pockets and rockin' bod and you forget all about me."

"Mary, No!"

"Lighten up, Soph, I am teasing you." I breathe a sigh of relief. I would hate it if Mary was mad at me. "Well, you and your wallet have a lovely weekend. I will see you on Monday, and I expect a full report!"

"Nothing in print!" I tease, hanging up. I roll over and smell Rhys in my sheets. Taking a deep breath, I pull him deep, wrapping myself in his scent. Yesterday I woke in an empty bed with a heavy heart. Today I wake in a state of bliss. How long can it last? Mary's teasing rings in my ears. *Mr. Money bags, you and your wallet.* She doesn't think I am that shallow? Does he think that?

I reluctantly slide out of bed and pull on a pair of shorts, as Rhys comes breezing in the door, sweaty and out of breath.

"Good morning, Beautiful. Sleep well?" His T-shirt, the shirt I stole, clings to his chest, wet from his sweat, and his shorts hang low on his powerful hips. Will I ever get used to how hot he is? He tugs his shirt over his head, revealing the chiseled planes of his chest, glistening with sweat. His abs pull and give as he tosses the shirt on my bed. "I went for a quick run. I didn't want to wake you." His mouth breaks into a wide, libidinous grin and he saunters towards me, prowling like a lion. Well, it can't be *all* about money. That body and what he does with it affects me so deeply. Wrapping his strong arms around me, he brushes my hair over my shoulder and kisses my neck, making my knees weak. I wrap my arms around his torso, wiping the sweat from his back, and revel in his embrace. Everything he said last night comes rushing back, and I am so happy to be right here, right now. I press my cheek to his sticky chest and breathe him in.

He tips my head with his finger and swallows me with a slow, deep kiss, savoring every second as I melt to the ground. When he finally breaks from my lips, I am bereft, wanting him to kiss me like that every minute.

"What is on your mind, Sophie?"

"Nothing. I just got off the phone with Mary, my boss. I was supposed to go in today."

"Uh oh. Are you in trouble? I wouldn't want you to lose your job….Again." He squeezes me tightly, and nips at my neck before letting me go.

"No. Everything is fine."

"Then what is bothering you?" How does he do that? How does he know when something is on my mind?

"Oh, nothing."

He drops his shorts and stands before me in nothing but his boxer briefs. They hug every part of him in a way that makes me envious. "Nothing rarely means nothing." He sits and pulls his socks off before walking into the bathroom.

"It is just something that Mary said." I watch him move around my bathroom, like he is familiar with the space. He splashes water on his face and reaches for a hand towel.

"What did she say?"

"She was just teasing me about your money." I shake my head, trying to shake off the doubt. "She called you my 'wallet'."

"Does that bother you?" He wipes the sweat from his body with the hand towel and drops it to the bathroom floor. He walks back into my room and sits at the end of the bed, waiting.

"I just don't want people to think that is what is going on."

"You don't care about money." The humor in his voice should be reassuring, but it stings, he couldn't even fathom that I may be so shallow. I am not so sure. It turns out that I do covet the things he can give me, the things that he has. "You only want me for my hot body," he teases me and pulls me into his lap. Oh, the feeling of being in his arms. That feeling definitely has nothing to do with money. Money cannot buy the way he makes me feel. The way he reads my body, that is instinct. You cannot buy the kind of connection we have built. Can you? How could I have been so righteous? Resting my hands on his strong biceps, I relish the feel of his soft, sun kissed skin under my fingers. I don't want to give it up. But surely he won't want me when I confess. Looking into his eyes, I want to believe that it isn't about his money, but the lie in my head bites my tongue. The silence seems to stun him. He balks for a moment, and wrinkles his brow. "Sophie?"

"I…" I don't know what to say. How to say it. *Hey, turns out it is about your money.*

"What is going on?" His grip on my arms is just a little too tight, his hands tensing in wait. My heart thuds against his grip. Blood rushes from my head, dropping like pebbles to my toes.

"What if…?" Is all I can muster.

"What if, what? What are you on about?" His eyes beg for an explanation, reassurance. Could he really care so much? He does, I know he does. The subtle shift in his embrace, the way he chews his lip. He cares, maybe more than he wants to. "Put voice to your thoughts, Sophie. Tell me what you are thinking. Speak up."

"I'm afraid that it is about your money." The words fall out of my mouth in a rush, and Rhys laughs. He pulls me into a hug, squeezing me around the shoulders.

"God damn, Sophie, I thought it was something serious. Don't scare me like that."

"No, listen, I am serious." I pull away from his chest and force him to look at me. To hear the words that could drive him away. "What if it is your money? What if I am just like everyone else, I just didn't know it until now. I mean, think about it. Everything we have done, everywhere we have been. It has all been paid for, owned or optioned by you. We have been surrounded by luxurious things, delicious food, no cares. You cornered me at a five thousand dollar a plate charity auction. That is not real life. Not for me. How could I not fall for you? You make me come so hard I can't think straight, put me up in a mansion, send me gifts, and show up at a moment's notice." My heart cracks with each word of truth. Saying it out loud makes it sound even more horrible, more undeniable. The words hang in the air, dancing before my eyes. "Private jets, cross country drop-ins. This is not normal relationship fodder for a girl like me. Your money has been a part of every moment we have had together." He drops his hands to the bed, white knuckled, bunched in the duvet. The whites of his eyes are larger than normal, and he listens intently. Watching my lips pass the words, the heat of his gaze burns my mouth. I pull at my lips, unable to shake the feeling that he is willing me to stop talking, to shut up. But, still I ramble on, tugging at my bottom lip. "How could it not be about that?"

Shaking his head, either in disbelief or denial, maybe frustration, I don't know. He stands, easily moving me from his lap, towering over me. His shoulders are set, his stance that dominating, powerful, squared-up stance that he does so well. I love that stance, love the set of his shoulders when he is in that mode, the urge to dominate and control too much for him to overcome. It's like his wild side. Only, it is so contained. He pulls me to my feet.

"Sophie." Winding his arms around my hips, he lays his palms against the small of my back and presses me to him. "Do you feel that?" His soft whisper sends a shiver down my spine that meets the spark between us and I shudder in his arms. Under the weight of what he wants me to feel, his heat, his hands. The way they make me feel, like I am falling and don't want to be caught, burning in a divine fire, dancing upon the flames, skirting the pain. "You can't buy that." He lowers his mouth to mine and flicks my bottom lip with his moist tongue. A breath catches in my throat and as I part my lips, he takes his opening. His lips are soft against mine, kissing once, twice, before softly exploring with his tongue and retreating to take a nip at my lips. I love kissing him. I was made to kiss him, he was made to kiss me. Everything he does fits me just right. He is right, you can't buy that.

I try to bury my hands in his freshly shorn hair, missing the longer Miami curls. The way they twisted around my fingers, begging for a tug. Now I can barely get a grip. And his cheeks, so smooth and empty, not a shadow to be spied. How precisely groomed he is when he is on New York time. I run the back of my hand down his cheek, storing the feel of his satin skin for a rainy day. He groans and pulls back, looking into my depths, his eyes warm and melt into soft, serene pools, and I want to swim. Struggling to wipe the worry from my face, it hangs there stuck, like a bad mask. I can't shake the feeling that Mary is right. He reaches for his pants, unceremoniously surrendered to the floor so late last night and pulls his wallet from the pocket, thrumming through the contents. A small stack of hundreds rests in the fold, enough to pay my rent, no doubt. And the card slots are full, my eyes going directly to the Black Amex. I have heard about those. He thrusts the wallet into my hands, clamping his hands around mine, closing my hands around the supple folded leather.

"Here."

"What are you doing? I don't want this!" The words tear from my throat in a gust.

"I know you don't. That is my point." Rubbing his hands over mine, I relax slightly, my hands still reluctantly wrapped around his wallet. "But, if it makes you uncomfortable, then let's put it away."

Stunned, I stroke the supple leather of his wallet and think. There is nothing normal about Rhys being here. Nothing normal about how I feel. Maybe we weren't meant to be…normal. What is normal? All of the luxury and opulence, crazy ex-partners, that is normal for Rhys. How is this going to work? How will he not find me immediately dull and move on?

"We won't do anything that you can't afford. OK?" His eyes are wide, swimming with mirth. My eyes betray the coolness I wish to exude at this moment. I want to shrug it off, like no problem. But my eyes jut from their sockets, bulging at the thought of racking up a tab with Rhys. Even when I am swimming in a pool of self-made anxiety, he teases and pokes me. "We have the weekend to spend together. How much money can we spend?" I know he is teasing, but the tally in my head is reaching the clouds with no end in sight. He takes his wallet from my hands and pulls open my top drawer. My mind catches up too late. And as I lunge for the drawer, my stomach lurches into my throat, wound in a strangled knot. The drawer falls open to reveal mostly panties and bras, but what is lying on top of it all is enough to make me pass out.

All the blood drains to my feet, heavy like bricks, while my head feels light as a feather. My cheeks burn, my ears crackle and I want to disappear. Rhys drops the wallet and a wide, devious grin cracks across his lips. He runs his long finger down the smooth, purple shaft, caressing the length, sliding to the tip of my vibrator. He doesn't look horrified. He looks excited. When Collin found my vibrator, I thought he would lose his mind. He was furious, took it so personally. He made me throw it out and promised never to have something so filthy in our home again. I bought a new one the day after he moved out. And now Rhys rakes it over. I am stunned into a searing silence, waiting for his reaction. First money, now vibrators, is there anything more uncomfortable that we could talk about? Just when I think the silence is going to swallow me, leaving a gaping sink hole to hell in my bedroom, he picks it up. Gripping it with his fist, he runs his hand from tip to bottom before turning it on. It rears its quiet little head, the pitch getting higher as he turns it to full speed. His eyes are wide, like a child at Christmas, when he turns to me.

"Oh, we have to use this." His grin wide and unguarded, a child with a new toy, a toy he wants to use on me.

"Together?" I choke out the words. I have never thought of my vibrator as a tool between two lovers. It is a substitute, a pinch hitter, not a team player.

"We'll keep that for later," he teases, dropping it and pushing the drawer closed, loving the shock that has frozen me in place. "Surely I will think on it all day. But, in the interim, let's do what you would normally do. What is on the agenda for today?"

"Well, I usually go to the farmers' market on Saturday morning."

"Then to the farmers' market we will go, Ms. Noelle." And just like that he drops the vibrator, shuts the drawer and closes the subject.

Chapter 5

We walk along the dirt path, winding between farm stands. Table after table is piled high with the summer's bounty, ripe summer tomatoes, gargantuan cucumbers and bunches of onions are draped over folding tables. Herbs of every variety lined up under the dripping tables, pots of basil and rosemary, mint and thyme circle prolifically blooming pots of geraniums and hanging baskets of petunias. The temperatures have not yet topped out so it's still comfortable to stroll and take in the variations. I love the farmers' market in the summer time. I always find something interesting to cook with, or some unknown pastry. There are butchers that smoke and dry their own jerky, cheese mongers that make specialty cheeses and coffee trucks that run the gamut from black coffee and a donut to French Press and elaborate croissants.

"Ten dollars for a tomato!" he exclaims as he stops dead in front of a tomato stand. The crates are filled with ugly Heirloom tomatoes in a dozen different varieties, Green Striped Zebras, Lemon Boys and Deep Purple Cherokees. But the one he holds in his palm is a Mortgage Lifter, and boy, do they live up to their name! It is plump and bulbous, weighing a solid four pounds and eclipsing the massive size of Rhys' outstretched palm. I take the tomato from his hand and replace it before picking up a bunch of Campari tomatoes still on the vine.

"Heirloom tomatoes are rare and harder to cultivate," I explain. "The flavor is unique and pure, they are well worth the price, and these are organic which makes them even harder to grow. I always buy my tomatoes from this stand, they donate a large part of their harvest every season. It's well worth it in my opinion." I continue to gather a rainbow variety of tomatoes and pay for them. "I am surprised you would be so…frugal," I tease him, walking past a stand selling local apples and peaches.

"I do know the value of a dollar, and the good that money well spent can do. Don't be fooled by the trust fund, Baby, it's not all daddy's money." His grin is infectious. I can't help but reflect and bask in his light mood. So relaxed and open. "I made my first million at sixteen." He grabs an apple, popping it off his elbow, and casually strolls to the next tent. I pay for the apple and follow quickly behind, in awe.

"Are you serious?" Baffled by the mere idea of one million dollars, at sixteen years old? Our worlds could not be more distant if I had grown up on the moon.
"I have always had a head for numbers and business, investments really. My father gave me a challenge, he loaned me one hundred thousand dollars to invest. I told him I could double it. Within a year I had paid him back, with interest, and made myself a cool mil in the process. I turned around and invested that, and….here we are. *Not* spending that money." His sharp tone betrays his playful mood.
"What did you invest in?" I'm unable to quell the curiosity, even though I know nothing about investing.

"Maybe I'll show you sometime." Grasping my hand, he tugs me through the crowd with a zealous grin that spreads from ear to ear. "I love this place. Look at those monster zucchini. Ooh, let's get a coffee." He pulls me towards the shade, under the awning of a food truck offering French pastries and pressed coffees. He twirls me around and hugs me so tightly, resting his chin atop my head. He speaks over my head to the woman in the truck. He orders an almond croissant and two espressos, planting a kiss at the crown of my head before we step back and wait. He pushes me back, extending his open palm, cocking his head to the side. "I need some money, Mama." Oh yeah. I forgot we were doing this. I fish into my pocket and pull my carefully folded stack of cash out, handing him a ten dollar bill. He pays and pockets the change with a wicked grin. We sip our coffee perched on the curb and share the croissant.

"I just have one more stop to make if you don't mind."

"Of course not, Beautiful, you lead the way." He stands and offers me his hand before tossing his coffee cup into the recycle bin. "Where to?" The lovely weight of his hand settles at the small of my back as he leads from behind.

"Just down the end there." I point to the end of the market. Amidst all the stark white awnings and clean looking farm stands, nestled between and herb stand and a stand selling homemade soaps. The white tent is hung over every inch with richly worn tapestries. Brightly colored tie dye T-shirts and shorts hang from every corner. Smoke wafts around the entrance and an oddly soothing musical gong welcomes you out of the hot sun into the over warm, dark and smoky tent. Behind a long table covered with altars and tributes, stands a short round woman. She is cloaked in a long, swaying broom skirt and layered tunics, her feet are bare. Her arms are covered with bangles up to her elbow and her hair is twisted in a loose gray knot at the top of her head. When she turns she almost loses her balance as the bells at her waist jingle and sing.

"Well, I will be a monkey's uncle! Sophie Rose, you get over here right now!"
"Hi, Roseanna." I let her embrace me and inspect me as she has always done. She is my Godmother and was my mother's best friend.

"You are looking more and more like your mother every day, young lady, so beautiful, so natural." She twists my loose hair between her fingers, running her thumb across my cheek with a woeful look in her eye. "It's almost hard to look at you." Before she can get too deep into a reminiscent mood, she spies Rhys and an unbidden grin cracks her narrow lips. "And who is this?" she questions, taking his hand into hers. Slowly, she turns his hand over and traces the lines on his palm, watching his eyes. He just smiles and complies, cool as a cucumber.
"Roseanna, this is my friend, Rhys."

"Lovely to meet you," he offers with his signature grin. She grabs his outstretched hand and begins to trace the lines on his palm.

"Well, now, Sophie. This is much better than that other *boy.*" She looks from me back to Rhys.

"This is a man. Your life line is strong, and your virility can never be questioned."

"You got that from looking at my hand?" his skepticism is hard to hide. She places his hand in mine before turning to grab a small candle.

"I did. I could tell you a lot more if you were to have a reading. But I can assume that little Miss Sophie here won't allow it." He looks at me and I shake him off. Her tarot card reading is nothing more than a party trick, and often results in a dire ending message for her poor subjects. She lights the candle and sets it on the altar of Venus. "This candle is for you, Sophie. Let Venus guide you and true love will surely reveal your inner goddess." *Damn Her!* A deep blush inches up my neck setting my cheeks aflame as Rhys chuckles under his breath. "Oh, don't be embarrassed, Sophie. I just want you to be happy. It is my job to help look after you. Your mother would have wanted it."

"Well, I just wanted to stop in and say hi, Roseanna. We really should be going." A long tendril of smoke swirls from a stick of incense she lights and plunges into a pot of sand.

"It is always good to see you, Sophie. Don't be a stranger." She pulls me into a tight hug, her arms wound about my shoulders. "You look very happy," she whispers into my ear before releasing me. "It was very nice to meet you, young man. Be good to this one, the universe is watching." She winks at him before handing me a short, white pillar candle. "Take this, Sophie, for your altar. Light a candle for your mother tonight. I will do the same."

The thought twists my heart in a tight knot. We always lit a candle for our heartache. It was something my mother always encouraged. She said the heat from the flame would drive away the cold and when the flame dies, representing its last breath as fire, it would consume the heartache and leave you whole. I haven't lit a candle for my parents in a very long time.

We head back towards the car with our take from the market and the candle for an altar I no longer maintained. *Would my mother be disappointed?*

After a quiet drive, I unpack and clean the veggies and fruit we picked up. I turn on some music and start to whirl around the kitchen. My ritual when I'm feeling low. Music and cooking almost always do the trick, distracting me from whatever is weighing heavily on my heart. I cannot get Roseanna out of my mind. In the last year I have really tried to dig myself from this hole of despair, to rid myself of the bad and focus on being whole again. It all started with kicking Collin to the curb. Granted, it took a couple of times for it to stick, but it did. But in the process, I shut myself away, avoided everyone who could make me feel sad or reminiscent. I have avoided Roseanna and she knows it.

I start washing tomatoes and peeling onions, losing myself in the process, barely aware that Rhys disappeared almost the moment we walked through the door. I toss the tomatoes and onions on a sheet pan and slide them into the oven to roast and grab an avocado.

"What are you making?" He winds his arm around my waist, catching me by surprise. I jump slightly in his arms and then settle into the warm comfort of his rock hard chest.

"Just some snacks for us. I thought I would make some salsa and guacamole and we can grill, how does that sound?"

"Sounds perfect," he purrs against my ear, sending a shiver licking down my spine. He spins me around and in his hand is my old altar. A small carved platform with raised reliefs of the female forms in various goddess poses. It is covered with colorful drips from numerous candles, hard wax dripping down the sides. A fine layer of dust coats the whole thing as it has been sitting in the bottom of my closet for longer than I care to admit.

"Where did you find that?" I bite my lip and fight the sob that sits high in my throat. Looking at it brings back so many memories, but most of all it makes me feel guilty, guilty for sticking it in the bottom of the closet, guilty for not carrying on what I used to share with my mom, guilty for not honoring her and myself. I stand stock still, watching him hold a piece of my mother's memory in his hands.

"I found it in your closet," his voice is soft and unsure. I snatch it from his hand like a little child and cradle it in my arms.

"You have a real issue with boundaries!" I snap, angry that he has snooped. "You cannot just change people's locks, break into their house and go through their closets." He balks at my reaction and takes a step back. In a silent standoff, I watch his face, the tick at the corner of his mouth, the way he pulls his lips through his teeth, anxious and unsure of his response. Taking a deep breath, my shoulders fall and my body bows under the weight of my growing guilt.

"I am sorry if I upset you, Sophie. I didn't mean to." He watches me and waits. My heart is pounding a tattoo against my chest. "Are you really angry with me?" I have never heard Rhys' voice sound so unsure, so remorseful. Every cell in my body is eclipsed by a feeling of sadness that I try to cover with anger, but it isn't working. I shake my head, but cannot find my tongue. Large tears form in my eyes, the kind that don't immediately fall, but well-up and slowly steal your sight. A breath hitches in my throat and a heavy tear falls to my cheek, opening the flood gates.

"Oh, no," Rhys gasps and pulls me into his arms, wrapping his protective strength around me. I bury my face in his chest and sob, unable to stop. Salty tears soak his shirt, but he just holds me. His hands run up and down the planes of my back. The repetition is soothing and I allow myself to just cry. Just let it out and get it over with. I cannot hold it in anymore, if I do, I fear I will break for good. I can let it all go while he is holding me, I can surrender to the grief that I have ignored for so long. I want to let it all go.

I couldn't say just how long we stood in the kitchen, with me wrapped in his arms, him calming me with his touch. But when my tears ran dry, the sun was setting, casting a brilliant pink light through the kitchen window.

"Do you want to talk about it?"

"No," the sentiment is heavy. "Let's just eat."

I push out of his arms and he looks lost. But I don't want to linger on the feelings that I let out. I just want to pretend it didn't happen. I ask him to go and light the grill while I finish the salsa and pour some tortilla chips into a bowl. Rhys is clearly shaken by my reaction. After we eat, we sit quietly and watch random TV that neither of us is very interested in while he holds me close. He just holds me, doesn't try to kiss me or caress me. He barely speaks a word. He just lets me be. I must have fallen asleep in his arms because when I wake I am tucked into the crook of his shoulder while he sleeps with his head propped upon his hand. I wake him with a kiss to his neck and a nibble on his ear. He groans and opens his sleepy eyes just long enough for me to coax him from the couch and lead him into my bedroom. He collapses on the bed in a heap and falls right back to sleep. I pull the comforter up over him and leave him to sleep.

I wander through my darkened apartment restless, listless, but unwilling to do the thing that I know I should do. I sit at the kitchen table and stare at it. It mocks me. The altar sits on the table, right where Rhys left it, calling my name. Wondering why I have abandoned her, why I have abandoned the memory of my mother. I run my finger along the edge and pry off a piece of old purple wax. It still smells like the oils my mother used to make her candles, rosemary and lavender. I reach behind me for the candle Roseanna gave me, turning it over between my fingers. This one smells like jasmine and sweet pea. Roseanna was always partial to floral smells, my mother always thought them too overpowering. But I love the smell of jasmine, it reminds me of playing in Roseanna's backyard when I was a child. The warm summer nights that she and my mother would spend together while I played, laced with the smells of flowers and sandalwood, they would watch me play and laugh. I could always make my mom and Roseanna laugh, though I never really understood what they were laughing at.

I take a deep breath, filling my lungs with the scent of Roseanna's candle, fighting the urge to light it.

"Why are you sitting in the dark?" his sleepy whisper catches me by surprise, and I turn to see his silhouette in the doorway. He walks over and takes a seat next to me at the table and pulls the altar closer to him. Running his finger up and over the rivulets of dried candle wax, he watches me and waits.

"Tell me about your parents, Sophie." I watch him and mull over the request, needing to unburden myself. I am restless and filled with an unexplained anxiety that can only stem from seeing Roseanna and bringing up painful memories. I know the only way to relieve the pressure is to talk about it, but I don't want to burden Rhys. I don't want the dark cloud of my grief to color whatever this is, whatever it may become. "Please," he begs quietly, "talk to me." I am resigned. I know I have to talk about it. I know I should be honest with him.

"They were high school sweethearts, together since they were fifteen." Just the thought of being with someone for so long and from such a young age boggles my mind, but for them it worked. "They were polar opposites, my dad was a physicist and my mom was an artist. She used to confound him, but God, did he love her. They were so happy." And they were happy, always smiling at each other, kissing, holding hands. They were so affectionate, towards each other and towards me. We were all so happy. "I was so lucky to have them. When they told me in the hospital what had happened, I thought it was a bad joke. I just knew that things like that did not happen to people like us. My parents were happy, they were good people, and I needed them. They couldn't be gone. But they were." He puts his arm around my shoulder and pulls me closer and I rest my head in the crook of his neck.

"My mom was such a free spirit. You met Roseanna, her and my mom were practically inseparable. My dad was so rigid, so logical, but he just got her. He understood my mom better than anyone, and she knew how to make him laugh. They were perfect for each other. My mom was my best friend, and my dad was the best man I had ever known." I sigh, but don't cry. Talking about them feels good, cathartic, healing. "I miss them." Rhys places the altar upright and puts the candle from Roseanna in the middle.

"Let's light this," he stands and grabs a lighter out of the bowl next to the door, "for your mom and dad." He sits back down next to me and hands me the lighter. "Do it, Sophie. You need to do it." I know he is right. I take the lighter and spark the candle. The wick erupts into a bright green flame, sparking and bending until it settles into a healthy, high reaching pillar of glowing orange flame. The kitchen is filled with a soft glow that radiates from the candle. Shadows dance across Rhys' placid face as a tear rolls down my cheek. He catches it with the pad of his thumb, swiping it across my lips before claiming my tears for his own, kissing me so deeply, lapping the falling tears away with his warm tongue. Grief drains from my body under the safe passage of his gentle fingertips as he winds his hand behind my neck and pulls me closer. An urgency blooms between us and the sparks of the candle have lit a fire that neither one of us can deny. My breathing picks up as his kiss deepens and he pulls me from my chair into his lap.

"Let me cleanse you, Sophie. You are safe." He speaks into my mouth without ever breaking the kiss and his words fill me. The empty space in my chest slowly swelling with a warmth that I had long forgotten. His kiss chips away at the last crumbling bricks of the wall I have hid behind for so long. And as the wall quietly crumbles to the ground, I am thankful to be in his arms. My whole body aware on a whole new level. He cups my face in his hands and stares into my eyes, those big green eyes filled with nothing but concern and pure longing. As if my pain hurts him more than it hurts me. He pulls me to his lips, a demand passing between us as he swallows me whole, "Let it go, Sophie."

I fall into the kiss and abandon myself fully to him and everything falls away. In the darkness, we sit. Our mouths dancing, arms tangled and tugging. In that moment, nothing exists but the two of us. I could not say where I end and where he begins and it is so overwhelming I don't know whether to cry or shout. I cannot get close enough to him as I crush myself to his chest, wanting to crack him open and crawl inside. I turn and straddle him on the chair, needing every inch of me to be pressed against every inch of him. Never have I felt so lost to someone, felt so safe and I want more. I need more. I will never get enough of feeling like this. One moment I was sad and the next I am completely swept away by this man who has learned me, who cares for me, who wants to take my pain away.

He pushes back from me and the fire in his eyes is delightfully startling. He looks consumed with lust.

"I need to possess you, Sophie, to fill you up, I will go mad if I don't," his husky voice tickles my ears and makes me wet. He stands with me in his lap, his strong arms wrapped around me as he walks us into the living room, gently laying me on the floor. "I want to get lost with you, Beautiful." He pulls my shorts off, the tips of his warm fingers running the lengths of my legs as he does so painfully slow. My head is swimming in a pool of turbulent lust watching him slowly undress me and then himself. As he stands and drops his trunks to the floor, I am overwhelmed with the need to feel him, to taste him. I rise up to my knees and look into his waiting eyes. He nods, putting his hands on the back of my head, guiding my mouth over his hard, waiting cock.

Never have I wanted anything more. The velvet of his shaft against my tongue is heaven. The salt of his skin the flavor I have been missing. I grip him tightly and work him over with my mouth as he moans. Always guiding me, his fist in my hair. I get so caught up in the moment I push him to the back of my throat over and over. I am insatiable for him, unable to stop, to get enough. As I speed up, I feel him jerk and he tugs my hair, pulling me away from his body. He slowly shakes his head and grins.

"Wicked," he mouths, sinking slowly to his knees. He takes my face into his hands and grazes my lips with his, back and forth, so hypnotic. My whole body hums a tune I have never heard. I have never been this caught up. I am not thinking, just doing, he inspires such freedom in me. He pushes me to the ground and hovers over me, his fist tightly grasping one of my breasts. He tugs and twists at my flesh, leaving it hot and red, the light in his eyes says he likes the marks he leaves, as do I. In that moment I would gladly wear his finger prints all over my skin, to tell the world that I belong to him.

And as he slides in and invades my body, I do belong to him. Mind, body and soul. I am so lost to this man in this moment, he is the air that I breathe. With every slow, deep thrust, he fills my lungs with the pure air of his possession. He owns me, slowly, deeply, completely. He watches me as we move together, our eyes locked. My pulse races while he takes his time. The length of his cock slowly torturing me, sinking so deeply, then retreating only to return with a little more force. In our own reality, we exist, only the two of us. A tangled mass of limbs and lust. Our sweat slicked skin binding us, our racing hearts working to keep pace. In this moment I am a free woman, so lost to this man that nothing will ever be the same.

Chapter 6

The morning passes too fast and he is packed and ready to go. He looks back at me as his driver opens his door. He drops his bag to the curb and marches back to me with a swift purpose that sweeps me away. Lifting me from the ground, he kisses me. A kiss that rings in my toes as he quickly sets me back down with a grin. "I will be thinking of you, Ms. Noelle, every moment until we meet again. And I promise to make that as soon as possible." He turns on his heel and disappears into the back of the car, taking my breath and my heart with him.

It is easier to bury my head in work now. I know I will see him again, there is no question of how or if, just when. And the knowledge sets my mind at ease.

***

I stare down at my phone, stunned. The rocking of the ambulance rolls my stomach and I feel sick. My grandmother lies on the gurney in front of me, still and vacant.

"She is unresponsive," the paramedic calls to her partner who is driving. She starts some sort of IV fluid and turns to me. Her lips move and I watch them, but I hear nothing of what she says. A quiet roar slowly grows in my ear and I am deaf to everything, but the most ferocious beating of my own heart. It sounds like a war drum, filling my head and tearing my nerves to shreds.

"Ma'am?" Like a voice in a tunnel, her quiet words erupt across the van and I snap my head up. "Ma'am, do you have someone to meet you at the hospital? If you need to call someone, go ahead." She nods at me and I realize I have been gripping my phone with white knuckles, staring blankly at the blackened screen. I know who I want to call, but I'm just not sure I should. He hasn't even been gone for two days and already I am in crisis. I don't want to bother him. I don't want to rely on him, but every fiber of my being is screaming right now, I need him to wrap his arms around me, to hold me together while I slowly fall apart. Before I can talk myself out of it, I tap the screen and call him.

"Sophie, what a nice surprise, I was just thinking about you." His voice soothes me instantly, the silk wrapping around me like soft hands. "Sophie? What's wrong?" I take a deep breath and words begin to fall from my mouth.

"I think she has had a stroke. I don't know for sure." I shake my head violently, as if he is sitting right in front of me, an eyewitness to my confusion and shock. "We are on our way to the hospital now," I whisper.

"Okay, Beautiful. I will be there as soon as I can. *'Charlie, turn the car around.'* Ok, Sophie. Everything will be alright, you just stay with your grandmother, I will wrap things up here and get to you as quickly as I can." The line goes silent for a moment. "And, Sophie, I am glad you called me."

"Okay." A sick relief washes over me at his promise. She lies in front of me, now hooked up with bags and an oxygen mask. Her face is vacant, not like sleeping, but empty. And I have a glimmer of elation growing at the thought of Rhys. Guilt blooms around the shock that still hovers in my heart and I am overcome by the growing waves that threaten to pull me under. Guilt at thinking of Rhys at a time like this, regret for not spending more time with her, fright at being completely unprepared to lose her, although she has been slowly slipping away for years. It all twists around me, squeezing me tightly, an uncomfortable embrace that I become numb to. As the ambulance pulls into the emergency drive, I feel my shoulders fall and I just turn it all off. Letting it all trail behind me, I follow the gurney out of the back of the van and down the icy green corridors, numb. After an hour of gentle interrogation by the admitting nurse, and my scribbled signature on an endless stack of papers, she dismisses me to the waiting room while the doctors are in with my grandmother. Wandering down the quietly morbid hallways, I decide I cannot be left to my own mind. I quickly type a text to Olivia, asking about their trip, wanting something, anything to distract me, to take my mind off of where I am.

Hey Liv! How is the Honeymoon? Where are you two?

We are in the South of France! Everything is so beautiful ,Sophie, but we leave in two days. Back to reality. How is everything going?

I debate quickly whether I will tell her.

I am at the hospital, Lola had a stroke.

My phone immediately rings.

"Sophie! Is everything ok? Are you OK? When did this happen?" Her flurry of questions rests on my shoulders for a moment before I can answer.

"She had been getting worse, but this afternoon I was visiting her and she just, I don't know, changed. She went rigid, blank. She started shaking and then just stopped." I take a deep breath and push that memory from my mind, not wanting to remember her like that, writhing on her sad little hospice bed, unable to communicate or help herself.

"She is wasting away in front of me, Liv. All withered skin and hair, wasting mind and body. She hardly ever opens her eyes and when she does, she doesn't know me. She doesn't know who I am. It's killing me. The doctors don't think there is anything they can do. I don't know what I am going to do."

"Soph, deep in her heart, she knows you're there. I'm so sorry I can't be with you. What can I do?"

"Nothing, there is nothing anyone can do. I will be fine. I have been through worse, right? I will make it through this. I am sorry I bothered you so late, and on your honeymoon. I just feel so alone right now."

"You are not alone, Sophie. I love you, and I will see you as soon as I can. Who can you call? You shouldn't be alone."

"I won't be alone, Rhys is on his way." Just the sound of his name is like a bandage. I miss him, but I don't want to make any assumptions. I shouldn't expect him to drop everything for me. We are undefined, on unsteady ground. I need to take care of myself, but I am grateful that he said he was coming. I am met with a long moment of silence before I hear her again.

"Well, things have changed a little since we have been gone." She clears her throat. "I am glad to hear that things are going well for the two of you. I have to say I am a little surprised, but happy for you." She is struggling with her words, but I don't have time to care why.

"Listen, Liv, I have to get back upstairs. Tell Matthew hello and I'll see you both soon."

"I love you, Sophie!"

"I love you, too."

I slip my fancy new phone, compliments of Rhys, into my pocket and head towards the elevator to take me back up to the ICU. It is torture sitting in that little room, watching a machine breathe for her. Multiple tones, alarms and incessant beeping pollute the air with stagnant noise. The nurses shuffle in and out, checking vitals, always offering me pity-filled smiles as they quietly pad in and out of the sterile little room. The green walls are starting to mess with my vision. Everything I look at is cast in a sickly light. I close my eyes for a moment and try to block out all the noise and all the smells of disinfectant, hand sanitizer, cold metal and new plastic. This hospital has hijacked every last sense I have, twisting me into a nervous, anxious, teary puddle of mush. I wrap my arms around myself for a little comfort, the only embrace available to me. I let my mind wander to Miami. The warm, heavy air, hot Florida sun, and Rhys' gleaming crooked grin.

He is the perfect antidote, even if only temporarily. In his arms, my mind will be nowhere near here. In his arms, my mind is quiet. I didn't have to pretend. I didn't have to think. It's heaven, a silent, familiar heaven. He is all I need in this moment, all I could want. The distraction works briefly and I surrender myself to scorching memories that pulse through my body, flames trickling through my veins as the thought of his deft hands and soft mouth invade my grief addled mind. I can almost feel his strong arms wrapped around me as I think of him storming back into my life just days ago, declaring himself so openly. Everything was different in that moment. He was so raw, and almost convincing when he refused to say goodbye two days ago. I drift on the thought of his inscrutable face, the look in his sparkling, worry-filled eyes. He was so adamant about not saying goodbye, and here I am, waiting for him to return and nurse my breaking heart.

I am startled awake by a symphony of alarms, shouting, piercing the silent night. Nurses rush into the room and I shuffle out of the way, dazed.

"There is a DNR!" I blink and desperately wipe the sleep from my eyes. Every machine in the room is going off. The heart monitor pierces with a flat line. The ventilator screams, the pump noticeably still, unmoving. My heart leaps into my throat as I watch the nurses. They move seamlessly, unplugging machines and resetting alarms. In their purple scrubs, the oldest and most senior among them carefully removes my grandmother's IV and the oxygen monitor that is clipped to her delicate fingertip and crosses her hands over her heart.

"I'm sorry, dear," she offers with a warm smile and a pat on the hand, before giving orders to the others and calling for the doctor to declare the time of death.

Anchored to the spot in shock, I fear if I move I will sink to the ground from the waves of grief that are building. Threatening to level me, like a tsunami. It is coming. The alarms blare in my head, and I watch my grandmother. Her heart is still, mine is breaking. The weight of a strong hand on my shoulder comforts me. The smell of citrus and salt water soothes my aching chest. I close my eyes and surrender to the hallucination, happy to be anywhere but the tiny hospital room.

"Sophie." A litany whispered from the heavens. The strong hand coaxes me, centers me, and I open my eyes.

"Rhys?" Reborn by the sound and feel of his name passing my lips, I close my eyes and say it again. "Rhys." When I open my eyes, he looks forlorn, his face is dark and wary, sleep deprived. He is disheveled in a white long sleeve tee and dark, wrinkled jeans.

"I'm here, Beautiful." He opens his arms and waits, offering me a place to disappear, a respite from the outside world. Without a second thought, I accept his offer of safe haven and melt into his strong embrace. He presses me to his heart, his arms wound tightly around me, comforting and protective. His hand fists in my hair, cupping my head so tenderly, it's almost painful. I surrender to his strength, and tears fall in a deluge. His capable hands allow me to bathe in the grief. I let it wash me clean. I sob into his chest, vaguely aware of his steady heartbeat and strong hands. They hold me tightly and soothe my aching heart. By the time I find my voice, his shirt is soaked, saturated with my hot, salty tears, the planes of his chest just visible behind the damp, translucent fabric. Resting my hands upon his chest, I press my forehead to his heart and listen for the steady beat, something to ground me, keep me centered. I find it and focus on it. Letting it pulse through me, the rhythm of his heart steadies my own. Once I have filled my lungs with the deepest breath I can muster, I look up into his waiting eyes, clear green, soft and concerned. Could he really exist in this moment?

Everything is crashing in around me. My fractured heart is breaking to pieces in front of him. He is the relief I need, and the painful reminder that will pull me down into the deep. I didn't want to bother him with my troubles, I didn't want to assume that he would be here. But, I would be a damn, dirty liar if I tried to convince myself that I wasn't happy to see him, beyond happy. I can breathe again. As I let the flood gates open, I realize the grief I have been tamping down, hot on the heels of my relief. It all floods through at once; grief over the loss of the last person I love, pain from the broken heart I had tried to bury, happiness from being enveloped in his strong arms, and terror at the thought of being utterly alone.

"I'm all alone," my voice cracks, the whisper is so faint, I'm not sure I said it out loud. The pain in his face is all the confirmation I need that he heard me.

"No," he insists, kissing me gently on the top of my head. A gentle kiss, before he sits me back down, turning his attention to the nurses that teem around the central desk of the ICU. I watch him with dead eyes, I feel almost nothing. The faint beat of my heart is all I can hear, it floods my ears, drowning out the life sounds of the remaining ICU patients. Rhys passes the nurse his card and speaks to her emphatically. He is quiet, reserved, but his intent and determination radiate throughout the ICU. He is commanding and it is soothing.

Chapter 7

Moments pass in a blinding storm of papers and instruction. Rhys converses with the nurses and hospital administrator while I stand silently stunned. The vague memory of being shuffled into the back of the Town Car is all I can recall as I awoke in my own bed, the darkness of the night swallowing everything around me, cradled in Rhys' strong arms. It takes a minute before everything comes rushing back into my conscious mind and an incredible weight crushes my chest. My body is racked by a bone deep sob. I arch my back against the force and press into Rhys' warm chest. With his arm around my shoulder, he pulls me closer, tighter. I cannot stop sobbing, tears trickle down my face and fall to the sheet below. I don't remember feeling this empty all those years ago when I lost my parents. This is a new degree of empty. A new mass of weight sits on my chest, threatening my every breath. A cold, empty stone crushing my heart, making it hard to breathe, hard to think, hard to *be.* I feel his face in my hair. He kisses my crown and holds me tightly.

"You go ahead and cry, I'm here to hold you and wipe your eyes." I am vaguely aware of his fingers stroking my hair as he creates a hypnotic rhythm that makes my puffy lids heavy and forces me back to sleep.

Everything is black. All around me, black is all there is. The smell of the black invades my senses, the pounding sound of the black echoes loudly in my head. I am surrounded and completely alone, overwhelmed by the weight of my desolation, crushed by the very void that threatens to swallow me whole.

I couldn't say if it had been a few hours or a few days the next time I open my eyes. But he is still there, right next to me, propped against a bank of pillows with his laptop on his knees. He taps away, his fingers flying furiously across the keys, his eyes narrowed and focused. I watch him, not wanting him to know that I am awake. Wearing nothing but a pair of boxer briefs, he is beautiful, like an angel, here to guide me through to the other side. His bare chest glistens and his wet hair tells me he has had a shower. I wonder when the last time I had a shower was. I roll over and look up into Rhys' waiting face. I wonder how long he has been watching me. Opening my eyes burns, my lids are still heavy with unshed tears, my face puffy from the river of tears that have already fallen. The sight of him fills me with hope. Hope that he can plug the growing hole in my chest. Distract me from this all-consuming grief that threatens to pull me under and trap me forever. I could run. Run away with him to New York and everything would be different. And in that moment I am committed.

"Will you take me to New York?" My voice is hoarse and quiet, my throat having been locked and fighting back sobs for what must be days. A light shines in his eyes before he wrinkles his nose and considers me.

"Absolutely, Beautiful. I will take you anywhere you want to go. You just say the word." Pushing the laptop from his legs, he rolls over and pulls me to his chest. "What brought this on?"

"I just want to get out of here. I don't want to be here anymore. I don't want to feel like this." Running a finger down his chest, I skip on the ripple of muscle under his ribs and let the sensation of his skin spread through me like a calm fog. A stone core wrapped in the finest silk, he is soft and hard and the perfect distraction. "When can we leave?"

"After the service in the morning. Are you sure about this? Because, I will make the arrangements right now and we will go as soon as you say the word."

"Yes, I am sure. Do it. I don't want to stay. I want to go with you." A consuming smile spread across his face as he takes my face in his hands and pulls me closer.

"I am going to make it my job to make you feel better, Sophie. You just wait." Our lips dance in a slow, languid kiss, my lips still full from crying and stung by his passion.

"I want to take a shower." I slide off the bed as he pulls the laptop back to him and reaches for his phone,.

"Ok, Beautiful. I am going to get us ready for tomorrow." I close the bathroom door as he rings up Nina. I turn the shower on, peel myself out of the T-shirt I have been living in and drop my panties to the cool floor. I flip the light off, surrendering myself to the darkness and step under the scalding hot water, pulling the glass door shut behind me. I let the hot water sting me, every part of my body cries under the heat and a strange numbness wraps around me like a blanket. I let the dark and the hypnotic heat pound on me until I cannot feel a thing. Surrounded by a dark steam, my senses are jumbled, my sense of direction guided only by the falling water. In the dark I can feel so much more. Every rivulet of water sliding down my body, the rhythmic beating on my sensitive skin, it all melts together washing everything away.

A slight sliver of light shreds the darkness for a moment before I hear the shower door open and Rhys steps up behind me. "We are all set to go tomorrow," he whispers before kissing the back of my neck. I bow under the weight of his lips, my knees swaying as I clutch the slick shower wall. He turns me around so the water is at my back and I feel the bar of soap in his hands. "Let me wash you." I stand still in the dark while his hands skate over my skin, covering every inch of wet flesh with flowery sweet lather.

"Yes. Please. I don't want to feel like this anymore. I don't want to feel anything." I hear him put the soap down, then his hands are all over me. Washing and spreading the lather, paying homage to every hidden inch of my skin. Between my legs, his hands slide behind my knees and he kneads my calves. I place a hand on his back as he lifts one foot and then the other, washing me, touching every inch of me. Covering me with his brand of grief relief, and it's working. There is nothing in this dark but me and Rhys, his soapy hands and my racked body. His fingers slide across my hips, over my belly and he cups my breasts. They heave in his hands, glad for the support and attention. Round and round his palms swipe across my nipples, as they reach for him, tight and aching for his mouth. Wiping the soap away, he takes me into his mouth and pulls me deep and hard. With a nip of his teeth, he releases me and the sensation rings down the length of my spine. Wrapping my hands around his neck, he takes my other breast into his mouth and laves my nipple with the flat of his tongue, twisting and twisting until he bites down and I cry out.

"Turn around." His low voice resonates around the shower enclosure and down my back. I turn into the water as he presses and pulls the muscles in my shoulders, covering my back with the heady flower scented suds. Around my belly and under my breasts, he rolls his hands around my body like a discoverer exploring new places, places now shrouded by the dark. We feel each other because we cannot see each other. I feel him more deeply than I ever have. I trust his hands and his instincts. His hands come around my back and slide down my backside, his fingers meeting in the crevasse, pushing a river of suds down my crack. Pulling the cheeks of my ass apart, he runs his soapy fingers over my hungry slit, back and forth, spreading soap and my sticky arousal all over.

His hands rest on my hips as he drops to his knees behind me. I feel his breath brush the base of my spine and then his tongue. He runs his silky tongue along my back before planting a soft kiss at the base of my spine. His hands slide down between my legs, seeking out the heat at my core while he kisses the dimples on my back. Sliding his finger beyond my folds he slips slowly into my body as he stands up. With his front pressed to my back, he pushes me against the wall and slides his finger to the knuckle.

"What do you feel, Sophie?" he whispers.

"You," I breathe into the heavy steam that has settled around us, "nothing but you."

"Good." His chest rumbles against my back and I press my cheek to the cool shower wall. Everything he does feels so good. The heat and his fingers conspire and I feel light headed, like I am floating. His hands cover me in a veil of quiet relief. Rhys spins me around and I flop against the wall, unable to hold myself as he wraps his arms around me and picks me up. I am grateful for the reprieve, my legs no longer able to support me. Rhys holds me flat against the wall and slides his long cock into me so slowly I almost lose my mind. Inch by inch, he sinks into me and wipes my mind clean. There is nothing but skin and water and the throaty sound of his pleasure as he takes me in the dark. Hot salty tears rain down my face. I taste them as they fall into my mouth and dance with the streaming water. I am grateful for the dark, for the chance to feel it all. Maybe if I let it wash over me it won't feel so bad. If it all comes crashing together the pain will get lost. The first wave sneaks up on me and I quiver and spasm quietly.

"Oh shit, Sophie, you feel so good. Your whole body is humming. I feel every part of you, Baby." Panting, he continues to thrust through until his pelvis licks at my clit and I am pushed over the edge again. Free falling in the dark, my eyes full of tears, my heart full of something else entirely. It feels so good. "Don't cry," he whispers and finds my cheek with his thumb.

"You feel so good, Rhys. Please don't stop," I beg, pulling him closer, sliding my hips up his body.

His hands grip my ass and he pummels me. Rocking so deep my heart swells and I surrender to the final deluge as wave after wave rolls over me, under my skin, behind my eyes, down my spine. Every part of me rings.

"Oh, God!" he cries through gritted teeth, slowing his assault until he has slid to the tip. He hovers there for a moment, his breath heating my chest. His hands wind behind my back and over my shoulders. A delicate kiss on my collar bone and he pulls me down on his angry cock. In one clean motion burying himself, he pulls back and slams into me again and again. I ride him with my back sliding against the shower wall, my hands gripping his powerful shoulders. He pounds against me so hard that my pelvis rings and I know I will be bruised but I don't care. The last powerful thrust finds him empty and panting against my neck. I feel his hand above my head, pressed to the wet tile. He braces himself as I cling to his wet body, still connected. The water stops and he pushes through the dark and into the bedroom. We tumble to the bed, wet and exhausted. A delirious giggle trickles from my throat as he slides from my body and that pesky emptiness comes quickly rushing back. But before it can swallow me, I fall fast asleep, curled in a damp ball against Rhys' chest.

My hair is a crazy nest when I wake having fallen asleep wet and unbrushed, while Rhys is unsuitably perfect, as always. I find as I get myself ready for what is to come, the pain is slowly replaced by a soothing numbness. I can find comfort in the numbness. I am familiar and comfortable with being numb. And in the numbness the rest of the horrible day passes in a quiet flash while I stand calmly in the middle, unaffected and untouched by what is going on around me. Rhys has taken it upon himself to handle everything, well, actually it turns out my grandmother had everything already planned and paid for. There is a little of that old fashioned, war time mentality. She has had a cemetery plot and her last wishes recorded since my grandfather died. She is to be buried next to him, across from my parents. There is no real money to speak of, just a couple thousand dollars in cash that she had hidden around her house. Most of her assets were swallowed up by her long term care these last few years. All that remains is the house and I am pretty sure I will have to sell it, but Rhys says I shouldn't have to worry about that now.

***

The Town Car pulls along the dirt drive of the little cemetery that is perched atop of the hill just outside of town. Gravestones from as far back as the late eighteenth century sit on the hill, looking down on the new residents of their sleepy little mining town. The day is cold and gray, a fitting send off, for both of us. A new, fresh grave sits just off the dirt drive. Rhys offers me his hand and we walk across the grass, between rows and rows of souls, hopefully at rest, before Rhys releases me into the arms of Father Don, my grandmother's favorite priest. I feel myself being passed around, as I move from embrace to embrace; the little old ladies that she used to play bridge with, the women she worked with at her church, and few remaining people around town that she actually grew up with. There were more people than I expected. I take my place at the head of the grave, safely wrapped in Rhys protective arms and Father Don begins to pray. Every face is so sad and pity filled, their eyes unable to focus away from me, the sad girl who has no family to speak of.

Rhys tenses, almost imperceptibly, pulling me just a little closer. I look up from my personal hell to see Collin slowly making his way towards us, holding a bouquet of neon daisies, wearing dark slacks, a wrinkled white shirt and a smug sparkle in his falsely sympathetic eyes. I don't even care that he is here. Looking into his face, I feel nothing. A comforting lack of emotion, he is nothing to me anymore. Rhys kisses the top of my head and is quickly gone. Quietly winding his way through the crowd, he meets Collin on the other side and pulls him away. I pull my eyes from them and turn to watch a butterfly skip across the tops of the gravestones in the next row. Clearly she is confused, or she would not be here. This place is no place for butterflies, but I watch her, focus on her slight movement as she flutters from stone to stone looking for sweet nectar. I focus on the butterfly and tune everything else out.

***

I see the flash in his eyes as he recognizes me, the slight twitch of his fist around those damn ugly flowers as he realizes what he has just walked into. *That fucker!* And although I want to pummel him, to mar his flesh the way he did hers I don't. I stand and quietly, calmly wait for him to approach me. For him to show me that he has some balls, the balls to actually show up here, the balls to step up to *Me*. That smug smile he has pulled from his pocket makes me want to rip him to shreds. But I won't, for Sophie.

"What are you doing here?" I question when he is close enough. "You are not welcome here." I feel a roar building in my chest, but I know to push it back, to keep my calm, that is what is important right now. That is what Sophie needs from me, control. I am in control.

"Me?" Who are you? Some guy she just met?" He tries to step around me and I slide in front of him.

"Sophie does not need you here. She certainly doesn't want you here."

"Listen *dude*, we have a past. You don't know Sophie like I do. I am sure she wants me here, she *needs* me."

"No, you listen." I take a step closer to him and he squeezes his fist around the already wilting flowers, strangling what is surely their last breath. "I know what you did to her. I know how you treated her, how you manipulated her and how you hurt her. Sophie doesn't need anything from you, and I do not want you here. In fact, I don't want you anywhere near her. If you come near her, or contact her for any reason I will find you. Now, you can leave quietly, or I can escort you back to your car. But either way, you are leaving." Fire rages in Collins beady eyes, but I can see that he doesn't have the courage of his convictions, if he has any conviction at all. Narrowing his eyes, he looks over my shoulder and I wonder if Sophie is watching. Through gritted teeth, he relents, tosses the droopy, last choice flowers to the ground and stomps back down the hill, muttering profanities under his breath.

I close my eyes and take a deep breath, casting him out, casting out the fury I feel at looking him in the eye, knowing what he did to Sophie. Knowing how he hurt her, probably in more ways than I can imagine. I stomp the rage down, fill my lungs with fresh air and go back to Sophie. By the time I make it back to her, she is surrounded by a line of people, waiting to again embrace her and express their condolences. It's clear, watching her that she is unaware of how much love surrounds her. These people loved her grandmother, and love her by extension, but she looks so lonely, so broken, so fragile. I wait until the last funeral goers have stepped away from her before pulling her into my arms. Exhaustion has painted dark circles under her once bright eyes and a solitary tear rolls heavily down her cheek as she says goodbye to Father Don. The coffin begins to slowly lower into the earth and she shudders, turning her face into my side.

"Please, let's go. I don't want to watch." Her body is weak and slight as I wrap my arms around her. We walk to the car in silence as a soft mist of rain begins to fall from the sky. In the back of the car she curls against my side, releasing a deep, long held breath. Looking up into my eyes, I feel her pain and want to take it away. I want to strip her of anything that will hurt her. To make her smile endlessly, to laugh and be free, but today she is broken. I will help to put her back together.

"Where to, Beautiful?" I hold her close and wait. Whatever she needs, whatever she wants.

"New York." Her answer sears my heart. I know that she is running, running from this heartbreak and pain. But damn if I don't want her to run straight to me. I want to be there for her. I want to soothe her heart, to wipe her tears, to feel her joy. I have so much inside me that I want to tell her. So much that needs to be said. But she traps me with those big green eyes and I am putty. I want her with me, away from here and away from him.

"Your wish is my command." I tell the driver to take us to the airport and text Nina so she can let the plane know we are coming and we are off. Away from Sophie's pain, away from Sophie's past.

Chapter 8

Almost the moment we landed in New York, I lost him. His phone started going crazy, a steady stream of call after call from the moment we hit the ground. But it doesn't matter because I am just glad to be here, glad not to have to go home to my little, dark apartment. I have never been to New York, this is my adventure. I have a pocket full of cash, a leave of absence from the paper, thanks to Mary, and Rhys, my white knight, sitting next to me. Darkness shrouds building after building as we glide effortlessly along the streets of Manhattan. The city hides in the dark and I am left with views of tree lined streets, shining under bright street lamps. Drawn drapes and lingering silhouettes dance down block after block until we come to a stop in front of a beautiful old brownstone along a dark and quiet street. Waiting for Rhys to end his call, I crane my neck and spy the gargoyles hanging from the corners of the squat three story building. He clears his throat and pulls my attention away from the shadowed, tree lined street.

"Here we are, Beautiful. Let's get you upstairs." He pulls me from the car and leaves his driver to unload our bags.

I barely register my surroundings before I am swept up a flight of stairs and laid upon a cloud. When I wake, the sun is prying its way into the room through a cruel slit in the heavy drapes and there is a note on his pillow.

Beautiful Sophie,
Leaving you sleeping so beautifully this morning
was a feat of strength.
I wanted to climb over you and slide into your
sleeping body, so deeply that you felt me in your
dreams. But alas, work called me away. Work is
the ugliest and most demanding of mistresses. I
am in meetings all morning, but Charlie will bring
you to my office so we can have lunch. Enjoy a
leisurely morning and I will see you soon. R

My first morning is a lonely morning. I lie in
his oversized bed for a long while and take in my
surroundings. Rhys' bedroom. It's not really a
bedroom though, more of a loft maybe. The space is
open, but definitely private from the rest of the
house. There isn't much to speak of in his room. A
few black and white photographs on the wall of old
New York City, a grouping of house plants and
indoor trees crowd around the windows of a turret.
This building must be old. Exposed brick runs the
hall and stairway as I make my way into the main
living area. It's so open and big and raw, so unlike
the perfectly manicured residence on Key Biscayne.
Shining Parquet floors stretch before me into a cozy
sitting area and those lovely turret windows. The
space flows right into a large open industrial kitchen
with stainless steel, concrete and marble as far as
the eye can see. A massive island anchors the
kitchen with an iron pot rack floating above head.
An old fireplace has been filled in and a group of
suede couches gathers around it forming a focal
point. The rough edge of the exposed brick and the

big soft sofas make for a perfect space to curl up. Bookshelves line the back wall and lead around a corner into a big, bright study with windows on three sides that look onto a private garden, which even I know is rare in New York City.

Pictures cover the one wall of the study, portraits, paintings and family pictures. As I look closer, I see a picture of a group of young, ginger-headed kids, one sticks out with his inky, black mop. They are dressed in white robes and are surrounded by nuns, the photo reads: *Catechism St. Patricks. A*nd there he stands, my little altar boy. Every photo on the wall is about family, and Rhys with his father. Graduations, celebrations, milestones, they are all here. But one thing is missing, his mother. I look up and down each row of pictures until I find her, tucked in the corner in a small silver frame. He has his arm around her shoulder as she preens for the camera, she looks almost unaware that he is even there. Before I can pry any further, I hear footsteps and Charlie appears from around the corner.

"Morning to ya, Lass." He removes his cap and tosses it to Rhys' desk before plopping down into one of the chairs and propping his feet up on a glass table.

"Good morning, Charlie."

"I don't suppose you are going to lunch like that, are you?" I look down and realize I am walking around in just Rhys' T-shirt. Charlie laughs at my blush as my whole body turns a lovely shade of rose.

"No, Um…Sorry Charlie. I'll go get ready." I scurry out of the room and up the stairs as he chuckles and calls behind me.

"No apologies necessary, the view was fine!"

I turn on the water in the open shower enclosure and pull Rhys'shirt over my head. The warm water wakes me up and gets my mind working. So many family photos, so much more to explore, and Rhys is waiting for me. The thought charges me and I scrub my body quickly, a picture forming in my head of what it must really be like to be with him; never seeing him, picking up the scraps of his day, squeezing me in between meetings. I knew that he would be busy, and I came here to get away, to numb the pain and it is working. Like a dull ache, I have learned to live with. It is there, the nagging hole that reminds me how very alone I am. Yet, every time I see Rhys, every time he touches me it's like he fills it up, just a little. There are so many responsibilities that I left behind to be here with him, and I start to regret it just a little. I shouldn't be running, and I should be standing on my own two feet. Instead, I feel myself leaning on Rhys more and more.

I work through my self-imposed guilt as I dress and prepare to see Rhys, to see the people he works with, and the people who work for him. They will surely see right through me, but the thought of Rhys makes me wildly impatient. His hands, his mouth, his voice, it all makes me very impatient and single minded. The weather has been hot and sticky, so I choose a loose fitting cotton skirt that just grazes my knees and a lightweight cotton tank. Standing in front of the mirror, confronted by the new woman that I am becoming, I am struck by a naughty idea, an idea that will surely keep my mind occupied. I shimmy out of my panties and toss them back in my luggage. That will get his attention!

Sliding into the back of Rhys' Town Car the cool leather licks at the backs of my thighs sending a shiver down my back. We weave through traffic like I have never seen, block after block littered with yellow taxis, black Town Cars and other weaving vehicles. Nobody uses the lanes or stops at the red lights. They flow of their own accord, creating their own traffic rules and regulations. A wild and seemingly chaotic rhythm of stop and go, honk and yell.

"Where are we going, Charlie?" I notice the traffic gets slower, the streets are narrower and the buildings reach higher into the sky. Old architecture and new sway side by side, scraping the sky.

"The Financial District, Lass. We are here, it's that building there." He nods towards an imposing gray stone building. Columns rise from the corners like a great Greek temple. The building stretches into the sky, growing narrow as it reaches towards the heavens. Charlie opens my door, offering me his hand and I step out of the car, feeling like I am stepping into a movie. I have seen New York City in magazines, on television, in movies, but here I am standing in the middle of the hum, The Financial District and all the globally important buildings. People and corporations hover around me and I have never felt so small. Charlie presses his palm to my back, nudging me towards a set of heavy glass doors and a revolving round about.

"Go in there and tell them who you are. They will send you straight up to Rhys' office." I look up the building and wonder how high Rhys' office is. I would assume his office is close to the top. Is he looking down right now? Could he see me even if he was? I turn to Charlie and thank him before he hops back in the car and glides away, being swallowed up in New York traffic. I slowly make my way up the dramatic stone stairs, my eyes fixed on the rising building. I am reminded of my lack of panties as a breeze wisps between my knees, sending air sliding over my bare flesh. The cool air rushes through my legs as I open the heavy doors and slide inside the grand old building. Behind a heavy stone desk a small woman sits, her silver hair barely noticeable over the top of the marble platform. Armed guards stand on either side of the massive desk, watching people come and go.

"Can I help you?" she squeaks.

"Um, I am Sophie Noelle. I am here to see Rhys. I mean, Mr. Slate." I stumble over my tongue, reminding myself I am in his world, that these are his employees.

"Of course, Ms. Noelle." She slides a bright yellow badge across the smooth desktop. "Here is a visitors badge for you. You take the elevator to your right. His office is on the twenty first floor." She motions to a bank of elevators and returns her attention to her computer screen.

I step into the elevator behind a dark suited man and press the button for Rhys' floor. The man's dark eyes watch me reach for such a high number after he taps the button for the fourth floor. Before the doors close, a woman dashes into the car, her badge rattling against her chunky coral necklace as she slips between the closing doors. In her mid-thirties maybe, her short hair is spiked and tipped with dark, blood red highlights. Her narrow rectangular glasses perch precariously on the tip of her nose. She holds a coffee cup in each hand and has a paper bag slung over her arm. Her tight vintage dress hugs her tiny curves, stopping just at her calves. The heels she wears are so outrageously high that I find myself staring at her feet, wondering how she managed to run in those shoes. She twists her foot in admiration.

"You like?" she asks. "They're new," she muses, turning her ankle, showing off her stacked pumps. She looks down at the badge in my hand. "Oh, do you have a meeting on twenty one? Are you here for the interview?" Before I can answer, the door opens on the fourth floor and the scowling man exits the tiny space, leaving just the two of us. She turns back to me, her eyes wide and friendly. "So, you are here for the interview?"

"Um, no." It takes me a moment to find my tongue. "I am here to see Rhys. Mr. Slate." She cocks her head to the side and then her eyes grow wide.

"Oh my goodness! Are you Sophie?"

"Yes."

"Oh, I feel so foolish. I am Nina, Rhys' assistant." I watch her face twist with private thought. "I have heard a lot about you, Sophie. It is nice that you are here. I have never seen him so eager to be away from here. He has been working like a dog all day to clear his schedule." She pauses only to refill her lungs. "What big plans do you have for tomorrow? Rhys gets so excited for his birthday, but I haven't heard him mention it once since he has been back. Usually he has me working point for so many different people, I hardly know what is going on." Pausing for another breath, she looks to me and gasps. "Oh, my God, he didn't tell you it was his birthday? Of course not." The doors open on the twenty-first floor and she exits quickly, motioning for me to follow her.

I never get a word in, as she quickly shuffles me down a bright hallway, lost in her one sided conversation. A glass enclosure stretches from wall to wall, wrapped around a large office. She pushes through a floating glass door without so much as a knock and declares herself, clearing her throat, "*Mr*. Slate." He swivels around in his chair with a smile across his face that stokes my fire and I am reminded that I am not wearing any panties.

"I found Ms. Noelle in the elevator. Why haven't you told her about your birthday?" She sets the coffee down and puts her hand on her hip with a sigh before dropping the paper bag and turning to leave. "It was lovely to meet you, Sophie. Let me know if you need anything." She waves, gliding through the clear glass door, down the hallway and out of sight.

We are sealed in a glass box. Every wall is floor to ceiling windows. He watches me as I move to the glass wall next to his desk and make the mistake of gazing out over the horizon. My vision tunnels and I sway slightly, pressing my palms against the glass. The height and view are vertigo-inducing and the ground ebbs and flows in my sights, rising up then falling back. I press my forehead against the cool glass and close my eyes, trying to regain my sense of balance. His warm hands on my shoulders pull me back just as my eyes and mind conspire to make me feel like I am falling.

"So, Nina told you it was my birthday? I will have to thank her for that later," he mutters, swiping the hair away from my neck. His breath washes over my skin before his lips sink against my spine. "Come." He pulls me to his desk and sits back in his chair. I rest my hips against the ledge while he rolls closer to me, closing me in with his powerful legs. "I am so very glad to see you, Sophie." Resting his hands on my hips, he licks his lips and sends a tingle trickling down my spine. His fingers caress my sides as he gently lifts me onto his desk. I let my knees fall apart. Cloaked in the flowing material of my skirt, a slight breeze skims over my bare flesh. I drop my shoes to the ground and lift one foot to rest on his knee.

"Why didn't you say something about your birthday?" I ask quietly. His long fingers wind around my ankle as he runs his thumb across the crest of my foot. My pulse picks up, pounding through my veins. His hand skates up the back of my leg and stops at my calf. He squeezes the muscle, his strong fingers softly digging into me, before he leans forward and places a gentle kiss on the inside of my knee. "What would you like to do?" I breathe, unable to hide the lust in my voice. I lift my other foot, placing it on his other knee. My skirt falls back, exposing the tops of my thighs, inviting a bite of cool air to wash over my bare pussy. I shiver as his hands run up both my legs, his rough hands sliding along my smooth, pale skin.

"I didn't want to put any pressure on you. I would like to have dinner, nothing fancy." He looks into my eyes as his hands slide up the outside of my thighs and I gasp. Knowing I have a secret, so excited for him to find out. "And then, I would like to have you for dessert," he growls, pulling me closer to him, dragging me to the very edge of the desk. As his hands wrap around my ass, my skirt falls back and his eyes grow in delight. I lock both of my feet to his knees, bracing myself against his strength as he slowly slides forward on his chair licking his lips. A low groan rolls from his throat. "It would seem that my birthday has come early." My legs instinctively come together as he pushes my skirt up around my hips. He leans back in his chair and lets his legs fall open, taking my feet with them. He spreads his legs, spreading me wide open in the process. Cool air rushes over me as I am exposed to Rhys. His hungry eyes skim every part of me before coming to rest at my glistening core.

I know how wet I am. I can feel the slick heat between my spread legs, feel his warm eyes drinking me in. I feel his hunger grow as he just looks at me. My heart is racing, excited at being on display, at being so bold. "You little minx," he whispers, leaning quickly forward, anchoring my legs open with a strong push of his hands. He dips his head between my legs and draws a long breath, pulling ragged air over my wet lips. Arching my back, I rest my hands against the cool glass of his desk and surrender my body to his will. His fingers split me open while the tip of his tongue dances across my clit and a low moan escapes my throat. He reaches up and covers my mouth with his free hand, looking me dead in the eye, warning me to stay quiet. My pulse takes off like a rocket as he grips my face and sucks my throbbing clit between his teeth. I scream into his palm as he squeezes me that much harder while the relentless assault of his mouth has me shaking and ready to explode. He pushes his tongue inside as I come undone and he laps every last drop of his prize from my body, his hand remaining steadfast across my mouth to muffle my latent moans. His eyes are bright with mischief as he sucks my poor clit through his teeth again just to get one last squeal from me before he drops his hand from my mouth and grips my hips like a greedy, starving man.

"Oh, we're not done, Little One." He sneers like a wolf who has just dropped his fleece and I grin in surrender, completely willing to be devoured. He winds one hand into my hair and the other hovers over my pussy. The fluidity of his movement is enough to hypnotize me, as he pulls my hair, slowly forcing me to arch my back and reveal my neck, his fingers slide into me at the same painfully, slow pace. His velvet tongue glides up my neck as his fingers massage me slowly. Each pass he goes deeper, resting his palm against my clit, while he suckles at my neck. A slow searing heat spreads through me as his pace picks up. Lick up my neck, push into my flesh. Lick, suck, push. I start to rock on his desk as he pulls my hair tighter, my back arched so fiercely, when Nina's disembodied voice breaks thru my lust addled purrs, ripping me from the moment.

"Rhys." She clears her throat. "Mr. Slate, Mr. Darby has confirmed for the party tonight and your one o'clock appointment is early, and on their way up." Rhys' black eyes narrow on my mouth, his lips twisted in frustration. Sliding his fingers from my sex, I feel suddenly empty and worse for wear. I whimper slightly as he rolls my skirt back down my thighs and straightens my hair. He pops his fingers in his mouth and hums before a wide grin breaks across his face.

"Sweet as ever," he teases as I hop down from his desk and slide my shoes back on. He pulls my hips and kisses my belly. "I am sorry for the interruption, Beautiful. We will have to continue this tonight." His thumbs press into my hips and it ripples through my lower body. "We will be attending a party tonight, black tie. You should go shopping." He reaches into his pants and I scowl at him. He best not be reaching for his wallet, lest the hounds from hell be unleashed upon him. He pauses, pulling his empty hand from his trousers. "Right," he murmurs to himself as I pat myself on the back for the tiny victory. He will not buy me clothes. I will not take money from him, and it seems he gets it. "You will need a cocktail dress."

"I could use a bit of shopping I suppose. Maybe I can find you a birthday gift, too."

"Don't buy me anything, Beautiful. Just wrap yourself. It will surely be the most pleasurable unwrapping I will ever do." He has given me an idea. With a fast, wet kiss and a swat on the ass, he hurries me through the door and down the hallway. He presses me into the elevator with a hard kiss. As he steps back, my door begins to slide shut as the adjoining elevator is arriving, most likely with his next appointment.

Chapter 9

Charlie takes me to Fifth Avenue and drops me off for a few hours of shopping. When I exit the car, I am excited, who doesn't dream of shopping in New York City, on Fifth Avenue, of all places. My pulse is racing as I walk into the first shop with confidence swirling about me and a secure grin on my face. The first tag I check shatters the confidence and drop kicks my grin into the filthy street. I look up, probably looking like a stunned deer in headlights, into the eyes of a most haughty shop employee with a very knowing look on her face. I fake a smile and head back out onto the sidewalk. Well, fuck. Now what? Maybe I can salvage the fun, all the shops cannot be overpriced boutiques with frigid witches for employees. Two doors down, I find a vintage shop, but as I duck into the shop I realize quickly that it will not be fun, and I will not be getting out of this shopping trip with most of my cash. Designers as far as the eye can see, McQueen, Bill Blass and Chanel, not to mention the mind blowing vintage price tags to go with them. As I stroll past designer shop after designer shop, I decide not to let myself get discouraged, there is no better time than now to treat myself. Lola would want me to, my mom would want me to. Why should I not just splurge? I am in New York, starting a new life, going to a cocktail party. I pop into a shop that has a series of sleek black dresses in the window.

The clerk greets me warmly and is quickly by my side asking what I'm shopping for. He is friendly and energetic and gay as the day is long. The long strand of pearls around his neck and classic Donna Karan shawl give him away. He sashays around the tiny store pulling dresses off racks all the while chattering about what a slow day it has been and how he has been dying to dress someone and then, "Bam honey! There you are, looking all…needy! Now what are we shopping for today?"

"There is a cocktail party."

"Ooh, a cock..tail party, you say?" He grins and winks before digging through another rack.

"I have no idea what I am supposed to wear," I offer shyly. "It's black tie."

"Girl! You aren't from here, are you? You wear a cocktail dress…to a cocktail party. I will find something fierce for you. I'm thinking something like….this." He swirls around with what I am sure is supposed to be a dress, but in fact appears to be a micro swath of black satin with red bondage straps crisscrossing the back. It must stretch, but how much?

"Maybe something a little more, I don't know, classic," he huffs, but turns and pulls another more substantial dress from the rack, just barely long enough to cover my butt, no thank you. Dress after dress, he pulls until he finally stops moving and asks me the question.

"Is there a special man that will be…removing said dress?" He winks, nudging me with his shoulder. "Well, in that case, sweetie, you are going to need something fabulous to go underneath! Mm, I have just the thing in mind. Classic." He winks, and disappears behind a velvet curtain, before returning with the most beautiful piece of lingerie I have ever seen, and I am struck. Delicate black lace, vintage feel, it is special. One of a kind and although I am terrified to try it on, I want it. I have to have it. It has Rhys written all over it, for his birthday. And, if I'm right, I'll have Rhys all over me, and just like that, I know exactly what I will do for him for his birthday. "I found you a dress!" he sings as he shuffles me into a dressing room and closes the door behind him.

Three hours later and I am standing on the curb outside of Rhys' townhouse when his sleek black car glides to a stop in front of me. He emerges from the back and takes my breath away. Wrapped in a dark green dinner jacket and a shiny bow tie, he makes my knees weak.

"My God, you are breathtaking." His eyes twinkle in the glow of the street lamp as he offers me his hand and spins me around. He gasps as I twirl and reveal the deep plunge that exposes my back to the waist. He runs his hands up my sides and they settle at the small of my back, his warmth spreading over me like the summer sun. The dress is perfect, and classic. The sales guy nailed it after two hours of trial and error. Sheer black lace, cap sleeve, plunging back and a long straight skirt, classic, chic. It was more than I like to spend, but to see that look on Rhys' face I would gladly pay double. It is impossible to feel anything but beautiful when he looks at me like that.

"What has been keeping you so busy?" I ask as he spins me around the floor effortlessly, his hand holding me firm against him, his hips swaying against mine.

"We have owned this piece of land for quite a while now, but haven't been able to develop it because it is next to a public school. There is red tape for days when it comes to building next to a school. Just this week the school has been put on a short list of potential closings. We want that school closed. We can have the land rezoned and it will free us up to develop as we like. That is why we are here tonight. The head of the school board will be here, I need to get him alone and convince him that closing that school is in everyone's best interest." He swings me out of his arms and guides me in a spin before pulling me back to his chest. "What is the matter?" I cannot wipe the scowl from my face fast enough and he catches me.

"It's not in everyone's best interest, is it?" He anchors me to his warm body with a press of his palm and sweeps me to the middle of the floor.

"Please, elaborate."

"Wouldn't it be better to help and revitalize the school, wouldn't that be in everyone's best interest? Schools are integral to a community. If you close that school those kids will have to leave their neighborhood and be bussed to schools outside of their communities."

"What would you propose I do?"

"Why not donate your land and make an endowment to the school?"

"And how does that make me any money"

"Do you *need* more money?"

"No, but I do have partners, and it is basic business principal to expect a return on your investment. I do a lot of charity throughout the city, Sophie, but this is business." I feel chastised and deflated. "The climate of public schools is changing. These old neighborhood schools aren't large enough or modern enough to handle the number of children that they need to support. But I am not in politics or policy. I am in the business of development." He winks and lures me away from my doubts with a sly, crooked grin.

"Now, let's talk about that dress. You look positively stunning this evening. I feel there may be something developing *here*." He smiles and presses into me, his growing cock pressed between us. His hand glides down my back and he cups my ass. Swaying forward, he dips and runs his tongue along my neck and nips at my shoulder before dipping me back and placing a feather light kiss on my collar bone. Passion surges through my veins as he pulls me back to him and cradles my head in his hands. His soft lips are full and waiting as he looks at me with such a force that I struggle to catch my breath. Just as his lips cover mine the electric charge pulses and flows across my skin and my knees are weak. When I finally come back up for air all eyes are on us as Rhys' cocky grin ignites every pair of panties in the room.

"Everybody's watching," I whisper as he kisses my shoulder, his arm tight around my back. His feet glide across the floor without hesitation while he lights me up in front of every soul in the room.

"Let them watch," he murmurs against my throat. His hand travels up over my hips and across my breasts, brushing against my nipples that reach for him through the lace of my dress. Resting his palm against my chest, he looks at me with the heat of a raging inferno. Down to my toes, I shiver and melt from his touch, from the force of his gaze. "Touch me," he seethes, pushing himself against me. His breathing is quick, his pulse racing. I slide my hand down his chest between us and cup him. He fills my hand and grows with every breath as he presses against me, pushing more of the pulsing proof into my hand.

"I want to rip that dress from your body, like a fucking animal."

"You will do no such thing! This dress cost me three hundred dollars." He smirks and brings his lips to my ear.

"I will buy you a hundred more, just so I can rip them off as well." A shudder runs over my skin as his warm breath teases my ear and I am lost in a violent momentary explosion. Everything stops as his words solidify and my body is electrified. I close my eyes to absorb the quick wave that crashes in my belly and pull my lips between my teeth to stop from gasping out loud. With no warning, he takes my hand and swings me away from him, rolling me back into his arms, pressing himself to my back and then twirls me around again, pressing his hips to mine. The fire in his eyes is dancing along with us, I can see the lust in his eyes as he pulls me closer. The rest of the party has been forgotten as we sway, locked in each other's embrace. He squeezes my hand and brings it to rest between us, his forehead pressed to mine. He closes his eyes and takes a deep breath and I mirror him, trying to catch my own. A subtle cough and a quick glance over my shoulder pulls him from our moment. I realize Nina is standing behind me, trying to get his attention.

His eyes leave mine and he very easily slides into work mode and out of the trance we so easily fell into. He is all business. He straightens up and smoothes his suit before running his hands down my arms, placing a prudish kiss to my cheek.

"And there is the man of the hour. Sophie, please excuse me while I speak to Mr. Housen. Why don't you go get a drink and I will be right with you." He dismisses me with a pat to my ass and a gentle shove towards the bar. Just like that, the spell is broken. Another moment and I would have laid across the dance floor and let him take me, and yet in a fraction of a second the spell is broken and he walks away, leaving me sodden and more than a little irritated.

I sip on a glass of white wine and watch him. He is cool and tenacious, immersed in shop talk with *Mr. Housen*, the man who so easily stole his attention. He looks up and I catch his eye for a brief moment. He tips his chin to me then turns his back, leading his companions onto the terrace and out of sight. Irritation rises in my belly and I am suddenly overcome. He dismissed me for the first time and it stings. Pushed aside and abandoned at the bar, I know he is doing business, but I am still bothered. No, fuck that. I am pissed. I don't know a soul here.

I am in a new city around a bunch of strangers and he just leaves me? Pissed feels good.

I surrender my wine and ask for a whiskey before making my way through the crowd. I wind between suits and dresses and head down a hallway. Rowdy voices cheer and I hear a familiar, panty melting accent float from a back room. It is set up like an old fashioned card room, tables manned by professional dealers line the walls and a large, ornate bar sits against the back wall. A large group of men surrounds one booming voice that is so familiar it crawls up my back and sends a shiver down my spine. It couldn't be.

"Well, fuck me! If it isn't the one woman I could never forget." His accent rolls through the air and takes me back in time. Flashes of sweaty skin and tangled limbs dance behind my eyes. A marathon of epic proportions, two straight days of base craziness. *Andrew*. He was the manager of a rugby club visiting for a Sevens tournament. I was completing my internship in sports medicine and assigned to the rugby tournament first-aid tent. Nothing about it made sense.

At the after party, surrounded by rugby groupies and party girls, he picked me. He made his way across the party like he was on a mission. I watched him stalk towards me, knowing what was coming. I was tipsy, but it only made me feel bold and I was more than willing. Something about him just made me feel like I could throw out the rule book and ride him till the dawn. And that is exactly what I did. Two days later, we emerged from his hotel room like two, sun-starved hermits. We never saw each other again and I was totally ok with that. And now, as he stands in front of me, I still cannot believe that it was me that night he chose.

He towers above the other men, lean and cut. Even under his perfectly tailored suit, the definition of his muscles is unmistakable. His long blonde hair is pulled back and a two day shadow covers his jaw. He has pulled his tie loose and unbuttoned the top two buttons of his shirt revealing the smooth golden skin of his neck, making him look even more scorching. His warm brown eyes twinkle and dimples flash in his cheeks as he smiles ear to ear before closing the gap between us in two easy strides. He folds me into his arms, pulling me from the ground so easily. His warm breath slides across my ear and makes me cringe. His breath smells heavily of liquor and his words are slow and measured.

"You are a sight for sore eyes, Sophie." I always loved the way his tongue rolled around my name. "This night just took a turn for the better," he mutters into my hair, before setting me down. With his hand wrapped around my waist, he leads me to the bar and introduces me to the men who surround him. "This, gentlemen, is the kind of girl that could steal a man's heart. You never see her coming and then all of a sudden you cannot think of anyone else."

"Andrew!" I press against his chest and it is hard like stone. "Really, don't embarrass me, please," I plead.

"Alright," he relents, tossing back his drink. "You just caught me by surprise. The last time we saw each other we had just worn each other out. Remember?" He winks and I know I am losing control of this situation.

"I do," I say quietly, "but I am here with someone Andrew, so please." I find myself almost begging. "Keep it friendly." How could anyone be mad at those dimples? He smiles at me and pulls me close to his side

"Anything for you, Ms. Lovely."

"Sophie." His purr is dangerously low and wild with anger. I turn to see Rhys' cold, black eyes assessing me and then Andrew, and then feel Andrew's hand around my waist.

"Rhys, this is Andrew. Andrew, this is Rhys." A cool tension flows between them as I take a step away from Andrew's side.

"We know each other." Rhys' tone is cold, but the look he gives Andrew is wild with fire. Andrew wraps his arm around me and pulls me into his chest with a squeeze and a devious glimmer in his chocolate brown eyes.

"Mr. Slate, how do you know *my* Sophie?" I always loved the way his Australian tongue rolled around my name, but now it just sounds slimy and rage inducing.

Rhys slowly winds his fingers around my arm and pulls me from Andrew's grip. The ridges of his fingerprints fresh on my arm, he wraps me swiftly to his side. I am the rope in a private tug of war.

"Sophie is *my* girlfriend." His drawl frighteningly slow and measured, making my pulse spike. I close my eyes and let it wash over me. *His girlfriend*, I like it. It feels heavy, but good.

"Ah, Mate, seems we share our great taste in women." Humor sparkles in Andrew's eyes, clearly enjoying making Rhys' blood boil. Their mutual revulsion barely held at bay by their false smiles. Andrew's eyes shimmer at Rhys' barely contained jealousy.

"It's time to go," he seethes in my ear. He expects me to turn and follow him, but I am not ready. I turn to look at him.

"I am not ready." His gaze is calculating, yes narrowed to coal black slits. There is a slight tick at the corner of his mouth and then he smirks.

"Well, Sophie, something has come up, and *I* need to leave. So, either you can accompany me, or you can stay." The challenging arch in his brow is telling a bit chilling. "I will send Charlie for you whenever you are ready." He is smiling, but his face is hard and cold like stone while he waits for a response. I know this is a test, that if I push, he will make me pay. How, I don't know, but it's clear to see that he has been pushed too far and is no longer playing. But I am tired of being dragged around, tired of being left alone. I know he wants me to go with him, obviously. And, I truly want to go with him, I *am* going with him. But the territorial behavior is begging for my rebellion. I want to push him back for everything that has happened, every little hurt. For Nadja, for leaving me alone, for acting like a jealous ass. I am almost unable to fight the urge to defy him, just to teach him a lesson.

"Aye, Love. You should stay for a drink. We could get reacquainted." Andrew sneers, and with that he has sealed my fate. Now I know I have to go with Rhys, for fear that his head will blow off. At the thought of being forced, I reach for extra courage to withstand his inevitable anger and step closer to Andrew, wrapping my arms around his broad shoulders, giving him a tight, too long hug.

"Goodbye, Andrew. It was so good to see you." His big arms wind around me and hold me a little too close as he buries his nose in my hair. Oh, he is going too far, and he knows it. The gravity of Rhys' low-lying anger pulls me from Andrew's grasp. I push away from him, backing into the safety of Rhys' arms.

"You smell even better than I remember." He stares at Rhys hoping for a reaction. "It was good to see you, too, lovely Sophie." He draws out my name with a wide, mischievous smile. "I hope to see you again. Soon." Tipping his glass at me he winks, setting Rhys in motion.

"That's never going to happen." Rhys pulls me from the bar, down the hall and out a side door. The heavy metal door slams behind us and we are left standing in a narrow alley, the next building hardly more than five feet away. Limos hover at the curb lining the front of the building. The light over the door is dim, as one bulb is out and the other quickly fading. But the light in Rhys' eyes is blinding. He is burning.

"You were too familiar with him. I don't like it." His quiet single minded declaration fills the cold silence between us.

"Well, tough."

"Excuse me?" He steps closer, towering above me with his shoulders set in stone.

"I said tough." Stepping closer, I square my shoulders, wishing I was a foot taller.

"You are *mine*, Sophie." His lip curls, and he looks savage. Black eyes shine through narrow slits and his menacing tone slices through me. His large body looms over me making me want to press back.

"I know that you are kidding me, right?" Unbelieving of what he just said. I am not a piece of property to be owned, I belong to no one.

"No. I am dead serious. You. Are. Mine." He says it with such conviction that I may have believed him if my mind wasn't screaming *Hell No!!*

"You are an incredible hypocrite!" I shout. "I am not a toy, or a piece of property. You have a lot of nerve throwing a fit about some random guy. I have endured the sneers at the wedding, Nadja's incessant interference, and all with a forced smile on my face. Now you are going to make me feel guilty? I have a past Rhys, just like you. Get over it," I declare, indignant.

"Why were you so familiar with him? What…..how do you know him?" Exasperated with his feigned ignorance, I shake my head and watch his face slowly fall. The fire in his eyes fades and is replaced by disappointment and realization. "You said you were only with Collin." His voice is soft, the fierce resonance falling into the background.

"No," I say, quietly. "I said he was my first." His eyes grow wide, his body practically vibrating now. "I haven't been with a lot of people, but I do have a past."

"How many?" he asks in a rush, unable to hold it in

"Why is this important to you? I wouldn't dare ask you that kind of question."

"How many? I need to hear it." We stand, staring at each other, the impasse stretching like an elastic band, ready to snap and hurt someone. "Please," he pleads.

"More than three," I sigh, looking deep into his worried emerald eyes. His breath hitches in his puffed chest and he goes rigid. A violent shiver shakes my whole body as I stare into his cold eyes.

"I want to be the only guy," he mumbles

"Well, you aren't. That is unrealistic and unfair, Rhys. Can't you see that?"

"Maybe, but that doesn't change the fact that I hate that you were with him. I hate that you have shared your body with him. That he saw you the way I get to see you."

"No." I reach out and grab his hand. "Rhys, nobody has ever seen me the way you see me. Nobody has ever made me feel the way you make me feel. And nobody ever will. I am more myself with you, freer with you than I have ever been, than I ever imagined I could be. Only you have ever really seen me, only you. You have to know that." His fingers trap mine and he tugs me from the alley, towards the line of waiting limos. "Where are we going?"

"Home," he declares. "I am going to fuck you until my name is the only name you remember." Need pools between my legs, hot and heavy while the breath catches in my tight chest.

"I thought something came up?"

"I don't care about anything but you right now. I need to feel you quiver around me, I need you to pull me in deep and hold me hostage. Nothing else matters." He nods to his driver, Nicholas, and he opens the door.

Chapter 10

Rhys' stride doesn't falter as he glides into the back seat after me. I sit across from him and return his glower. His nostrils flare like a bull as we pull away from the curb. Streaks of light cross his face, the streetlights casting shadows, making him look dangerous and dark. I steel myself and sit back against the seat, watching him as he silently watches me. Block after block we coast past the street lights and he remains in the shadows, his silence growing hot and impatient. I squirm ever so slightly and his eyes flash with the excitement of a hunter who has finally spotted the weakness in his prey.

"Come here." He extends his finger and beckons to me, letting his legs fall open. The timbre in is voice is low and cold and my core is hot. I watch him for a moment, his dark eyes sparkle as he raises an eyebrow and points to the ground between his legs. "I said, come *here*. Now."

"No," I say. He narrows his eyes at me while a long shadow stretches across his face, shrouding everything but his wicked grin. He purses his lips in thought, before releasing a rush of air and he chuckles. Resting a loose fist in his lap, he pulls my attention away from his face. His erection is protesting his pants, he stretches his fingers over his growing bulge, pulling at himself, tugging his pants tightly, the outline of his cock calling to me like a popsicle on a hot summer day.

"Did you say *No*?" Squaring my shoulders, I sit back against the seat and shake off his first attempt to rattle me, and taunt him with silence. The dark slits of his eyes flare as we pass under a streetlight before he again escapes into the dark. His deep voice is soft, and his intention is clear, intimidation. His serious tone sends a shiver down my back and I am thankful for the dark, when he leans forward into the light. "You mean to tell me that you are going to get me all worked up, tease me, make me jealous, *on purpose*, and then say no to me?" He is indignant, clearly shocked, but is he shocked by me or by his reaction. He is the one who is acting like a child, not me. He puffed his chest and tried to bend me to his will. I was just saying hello to an old friend.

"Absolutely." I lean forward meeting him in the middle. His warm breath slides over my mouth we are so close, but we are in a standoff. Neither of us moves an inch, we just hover, our mouths reaching for one another, but our minds twisted in a petty war. He tugs at his bottom lip and I want to bite it. I want to jump across the car and let him take me. It is so hot in the car, the air so thick with tension and excitement that I want to strip down and ride him until he is empty, but I fight it. With everything that I have, I fight it. If I give in so easily when he is being so unreasonable, I will never again have control. I have to remain in charge of my life, he will not intimidate me. He leans back and assumes the dark again, hiding his face as he speaks in an even, monotone timbre.

"You are making a bid for control, Ms. Noelle, which is all fine and good, believe me, I enjoy a good row. But I will win. Yes, I may be an incredible hypocrite, but I am also a man. A man who has earned the right to take what is his." My thighs twist against one another, hot and slick with my wanton lust for the brute in front of me. I am supposed to be standing up to him, yet instead I find myself exhilarated and flushed with a longing that threatens my very sanity.

"I will have you on your knees, and you will go there willingly, eagerly." He sneers and I want to slap him, and then kiss him. Damn it! Why is he being such an ass and why am I not fighting back? It's his arrogant insistence that he will prevail, his confidence makes him almost unstoppable, almost. In me, he has created a monster. I know that he wants me. I can see it in his face, all over his body. I believe him, almost easily, when he tells me how much he wants me now. And in making me feel so sexy, he has made me feel powerful, powerful enough to resist him. "I need you to understand what has happened tonight, Sophie. You played with me, you made me jealous. I do not like feeling jealous. I would gladly throw you over my knee, but somehow I don't think that would work with you. No, I think something else is in order. In order for me to feel *satisfied*, that you understand the gravity of the situation, you will need to kneel at my feet. That will make me feel better." I laugh before any other emotion can reveal itself, a full on belly laugh at his audacity, his cool declaration that I will kneel at his feet.

"I will do no such thing," I declare before he even finishes. "You have gone too far, Rhys. Why would you want to humiliate me like that, to demean me for your pleasure?"

"Sophie, it is not about humiliation or demeaning you. It is about showing you how deeply I desire you. You make me feel so out of control sometimes. I need you to let me…I need you to trust me."

"How am I supposed to do that when you turn into such a bully? When you demand that I *submit*? You must know that all I want to do when you demand things from me is to defy you. It's like a knee jerk reaction."

"Of course I know, I like pushing you, I like it when you try to fight me."

"You like it when I lose."

"I like it even more when you win."

"That never happens."

"It happens more often than you think."

"It isn't fair. I try to stand up to you, but you don't play fair. If I felt we were on a level playing field, maybe I wouldn't feel the need to push back so often. I like surrendering to you, Rhys, but when it is *my* choice. Not when you demand it of me. It makes me feel like nothing more than a plaything."

"You *are* my plaything, Sophie." He leers at me across the car as Nicholas opens the door and he pulls me up the steps. We are up the second flight of stairs, and into the large master bedroom before I pull my hand from his. He pulls his tie off, flinging it to the ground and starts pulling at the buttons on his shirt. I step out of my shoes before walking into the large closet, hoping for a second alone, but he is right behind me, his sweet breath sliding down my back, teasing my shoulders and inflaming my anxious blood.

"Please, Rhys, don't make me feel cheap." I am ashamed of my weak constitution, of the fact that I have to beg for mercy, at the fact that I let myself feel this way. The hardness falls quickly away from his features as he steps close to me, his big hands easily wound loosely around my upper arms.

"I am sorry to the depths of my soul if I have made you ever feel cheap, Sophie. I would never want to make you feel like that." His hands circle around my back and he pulls me gently to his chest. He quietly undoes the satin bow at my back. "I just want you to understand how strong my feelings are for you. I desire you from the moment I wake up to the moment I fall asleep with you in my arms. Hell, I desire you in my sleep. I just feel so out of control with you, so completely taken over. I could drown in you sometimes and that is frightening. And then tonight, you pushed me, I saw you with Andrew and I just lost it. I tried to stay calm, to know that I had no right to feel what I was feeling. But I did feel it."

"What did you feel?" I ask, like a child anticipating the next page in a story book, while his warm hands slip under the fabric of my dress at the base of my spine and slide across my needy flesh. My dress falls to the floor and he stands back, gazing at me like a rising star. Lace top stockings and a lace brief are all the dress would allow and I am exposed. His eyes graze my nipples as they spill forward. And then his eyes meet mine and I am lost in his desperate need for me.

"That you belong to me, that you are mine and nobody else's. I cannot accept the thought of you with anyone else, it makes me crazy. I want you to show me that you feel the same way. I want you to feel as powerless as I do. I am powerless, Sophie. You have me on my knees." He runs his thumb across the top of my stocking. A breath catches in my throat as his eyes meet mine.

"What do you want from me, Rhys?" I am practically panting and all but given up the fight.

"I want you on your knees." His firm hand is locked around my shoulder, but I sink to the ground under the weight of my own desire to do so. His hard cock juts straight from his body, pressing against the fine fabric of his slacks. He reaches around the back of my neck with one hand while his other hand makes work off his belt and his pants fall to the floor. He pulls his impressive erection from his boxer briefs and it bobs inches from my face, and I am overtaken with starvation. It is the ravenous hunger, the sudden dryness in my throat, that keeps my knees weighted to the cold, hard floor. My mouth feels so empty as I lick my lips, watching his hand glide up and down his silky steel shaft. He stops and watches me, hungry and wild for him. Watching him touch himself is one of the most amazing things I have ever seen. The tension in his forearm pulsing as he holds himself just right, his body is so raw and masculine. The planes of muscle like sharp carved trails, perfect for my tongue to follow over the dips and curves of his salty skin. I want to reach out and touch him, take him in my mouth and let him slide to the back of my throat. But I wait.

His tip glistens as he takes a step closer to me, holding himself out to me. "Would you like a taste?" His husky whisper puts me in a trance and I gladly lean forward, running my tongue across the tip, laving away the glistening liquid that oozes from his beautifully engorged head. The slit wet with my spit, I part my lips and kiss the head, pulling air into my mouth, pulling cool air over his hot cock. He grits his teeth, pulling in a sharp breath before a glimmer flashes in his eye.

"Good girl, Sophie. Now, lean back and put your hands on your legs." He steps closer to me, practically bending me with his body. I lean back and rest my palms on my calves, my head tipped to the ceiling. As he moves closer, he hovers with my chest between his thighs and looks down upon me. "You are so beautiful. God, I swear I will never get enough. Open your mouth." I let my lips fall open as he probes my mouth, pressing gently against my lips and then pulling back. Bending his knees, he sinks all the way to the back of my throat then pulls back again. This angle, his hips, it is designed for maximum depth, I can take it. And I want more. I let my lips go lax and my head roll back, opening my throat.

"Yes," he hisses, sinking to the back of my throat again. A slight gag reflex threatens, but I push it away and let my head fall back a little more, taking him all the way to his root. "So deep, Sophie. You have all of me in that sexy mouth of yours." His voice slices between his teeth as he sets a rhythm of slow retreat and deep thrusts. He fucks my mouth while I lean on my legs, my thighs begin to burn but I don't care. I hollow my cheeks, pressing my tongue along the bulging vein raging up his long shaft. Watching his face is the sexiest thing I have ever witnessed. His twisted, flaming features unable to hide the sheer pleasure he feels, as he presses his cock into my mouth is intoxicating. Watching him take so much pleasure with me makes my blood boil. My whole body is on fire, my core is so wet, heat floods the air around me and my thighs are slick and sticky with my own need. He looks down at me and we lock eyes. I know any second I will surely combust from the electricity and lust that flows between us as he slides along my tongue like silk, his intense glare full of pleasure and awe.

His hand snakes out and he loosely wraps his fingers around my neck, his thumb coming to rest at the base of my throat as he thrusts deeper than ever. My eyes begin to water as he slides into my mouth, over and over again, but I relish it all, the taste of his skin, the feel of his steel, the burn in my legs. It all collides in a fury of excitement as he presses himself again to the back of my throat and stills.

"I can't last, Sophie," he pants. I move my tongue across the base of his erection and reach out to tickle his balls with the tip of my tongue when he pulls back and quickly slides himself back into my waiting mouth, quickly coating my throat with his hot seed. I let it slide down my throat, three long hot spurts, while he quakes in front of me. I let go of my legs and put my hands on his hips, licking his still twitching shaft from top to bottom, running my tongue over the engorged, sensitive skin until he is clean. Leaning back, I look up into his eyes and they are filled with something dangerous and delightful.

He pulls me from my knees, crushing me to his chest and our lips collide. Covering my mouth with his, he slowly devours me, his tongue washing across my lips, into my mouth and around my tongue.

"Mm mm. I can taste myself on your lips." His lips don't leave mine as he speaks, tugging my bottom lip between his teeth. "You are a wicked creature," he says, dragging his thumb across my lips. Before I know what is happening, he throws me over his shoulder and makes his way back into the bedroom. I squeal in delight as he slaps my ass, a deliciously violent crack fills the air, making me shiver. His hand runs the length of my spine, raising goose bumps in its wake. All the while a low growl rumbles in Rhys' chest, his back rolling with the vibration; I press my breasts to his back and wrap my arms around his hips. He slides a finger between my legs and beneath the scrap of lace that covers me and I moan, my hot breath sliding against the tight flesh that wraps Rhys' hips. Sliding a second finger into the fire, he steadies my legs and rocks me forward as he pushes into me, his fingers curled to press on the very spot that will make everything go black, releasing me into a divine oblivion.

He presses his fingers down to the knuckle, then slaps my flesh again, sending a shock straight to my core. I gasp against his back and squeeze him tighter, holding on for dear life as a wave takes me under. I am light headed from hanging upside down, my blood has been singing for too long, skipping on a high note, begging for relief. He presses into me and fireworks explode behind my eyes, making me scream out. Unable to hold back, I am left shaking, and raw. He swings me to the bed, instantly covering me with his sweat slicked body.

"You like that, Sophie. You continue to surprise me. Every time I fear I have pushed you too far you surprise me. Your body is begging for more." He dips his head and lays a leisurely kiss on my lips before moving to my neck and down my throat. "So surprising," he murmurs into the hollow of my throat, before filling the empty space with his warm tongue. Burying my fingers in his growing hair, I tug his head back.

"You have been holding back," I accuse. With a lusty stare and a swipe of his tongue across those full lips, I forget to take a breath.

"I will continue to hold back with you, Beautiful. I just forgot myself for a moment, forgot who I was dealing with."

"What does that mean?" It barely escapes my lips, softer than a whisper before he slides down my body.

"Nothing, never you mind." Using his tongue, he circles one nipple while his fingers tug at the other. A slow heat rolls down my body, through my veins and across my heated, sticky skin.

"I can handle it. I want it." I am practically panting as he makes slow work of my body.

"I know you do. I know you can. It's not that. It is what comes after." His chest rumbles slightly as he presses up on his hands again, hovering above me. He presses a finger to my lips. "No more talking." With the shake of his head, I stay silent as he settles between my legs, pulling my panties off and tossing them to the floor. One quick look and a crooked grin flashes across his lips before he hollows his cheeks, sucking my swollen clit into his mouth and my vision goes black.

He strokes my swollen folds with his tongue. My flesh begs for more and I writhe in an amazing, beautiful agony. Needing the release, knowing an explosion of epic proportions in eminent, yet wanting to feel just like this for so much longer. Hovering at the top of the note, my body keeps rising, step by step, hanging right at the edge. He slides his fingers between my lips and presses my clit with his palm, grinding against me, sending fire rushing through my veins.

A finger slips along my seam and he circles the tight bud, pressing gently against the ring of my ass. The breath catches in my chest for less than a second before I know that I want him to do it. In the next second my hips press down against him, pressing my tight, virgin ring to his finger, wanting him to break that last barrier. My body is practically crying for it, begging for him to crest that last barrier. He slides his finger back up to my wet pussy before sliding back down and pressing slowly beyond the puckered ring, straight to my dark soul. He pulls his finger back and then presses in again, slowly pushing until my body relaxes and I pull him into me. To the knuckle he sinks his finger and pumps in and out of my body, driving me upwards, filling me exquisitely, my body screaming in ecstasy. A high pitched mewl rips from my throat as I am pushed so quickly from my long suffering precipice that I forget how to fall. My heart is in my throat, my eyes are blind and my body hums at the highest frequency. This amazing life changing orgasm rolls over me in a never ending parade of release after release, sucking the very life from my body, until I can hardly find the strength to breathe. He lets my body fall to the bed, but before I can recover, he fills me with his rock hard cock.

"Ahh!" I cry out, my body screaming now, so sensitive, on fire and quickly turning to cinders. He pulls back and drops his hips.

"Open your eyes, Sophie," he growls. I open my eyes, and if looks could make a woman cum, surely that would do it. His eyes are on fire and burning right through me. "I want to watch your eyes." He slams into me and the force rings across the room. Again and again, he buries himself deeper until I cry out. "Come with me!" he yells, his eyes locked on mine. He raises up on his knees, his fingers digging into my hips, with one ferocious thrust we crash into each other and collapse together. His eyes grow wide and black as the deepest recess of space, and I feel as if he is looking right into my soul. A tear streaks down my cheek, surely from exhaustion, as I blink up at him, almost unable to withstand the very gravity of his stare. Our bodies twitch and struggle together, twisted around one another as we slowly return to earth.

Rhys releases a deep breath and his eyes narrow and warm before he slips from my grasp and rolls onto his side, leaving a hand behind pressed to my belly, which still rings from the force of his hips. Aftershocks rack my body and all the while I watch him, his dark eyes and their hunger barely sated.

That was a power struggle of epic proportions and still he looms. Who is to be the winner? Surely, he thinks he has won, as I lay spent while he watches me triumphantly. But I know better. I have won. I was never going to see Andrew again. And now Rhys understands how it feels to have to deal with someone else's past.

"You should make me a sandwich," I mutter as I roll onto my tummy and bury my face in the pillow, hiding the crooked smirk on my face. Rhys covers me with his body, wrapping his arms around my shoulders. His soft lips rain kisses on the sensitive flesh of my back, sending a shiver down my spine. His lips hover behind my ear.

"I will gladly make you anything you like, Ms. Noelle," he sighs before leaving me with a soft kiss.

I must have dozed for a few minutes and when I wake it's to a peanut butter and jelly sandwich. Rhys' eyes shine as he smiles down on me and the room is filled with lust and infatuation and something so pure. I prop myself against the wall of pillows and offer him half of the sandwich he made for me.

"What do you normally do on your birthday?"

"Questionable things, in exotic locations." His eyes twinkle as he winks and licks a bit of jelly from the corner of his mouth.

"And this year?"

"This year I will be doing very questionable things," his low voice rumbles through my core and heat floods between my legs, "in the most exotic location." His fingers brush against my pussy, still plump and pink, sending a jolt of lightening down to my toes. "My favorite place," his lips are warm against my neck, "a very exclusive location." He slips his hand between my legs and cups my pussy in his palm, sliding a finger beyond my folds, swiping at my clit.

"You are insatiable," I whisper, letting my head fall back while the sensation of his fingers washes over me.

"For you," he breathes before sweetly taking my lips.

"What is this?" I ask, unable to hold back. Our fingers laced, his strong arms cradling me against his chest, the beat of his heart a hypnotic melody. I bury my nose in his sticky matted chest hair and breathe deeply. Wanting the scent of him seared into my memory. Everything feels suddenly different, settled. I cannot continue to merely orbit around him, pushed and pulled by his whims. I need and deserve a little clarity.

"Hmmm?" He traces circles on my shoulder with his finger, leaving trails of heat with every feather light stroke, his lips softly resting at the top of my head. Relaxed and sated, his demeanor is markedly different. His touch lush, and slow, the immediate need for control calmed. He is unguarded, generously so. "This….is amazing," he mutters.

I press my cheek against his chest while he runs his hands along the dips and curves of my back and shoulders, kneading and pressing. The room is quiet, but for our breathing. The air is still, but for his gentle movements upon my skin. My mind is peaceful. In his arms, I find it easier and easier to quiet the disbelief, the feeling that at any moment I may wake up and be left standing, still alone, and broken. There has been a seismic shift between us. We finally understand one another, if only for a moment. My heart is full, as are my arms. The silence is crackling between us, perfect and still. The constant beat of New York City is a distant reminder that we are not alone.

Chapter 11

The morning proves the quick comfort we have developed as he readies for work and I watch.

"You lying there like that is very unfair, Beautiful." I turn under the light comforter as a strategic corner slips, revealing flesh to the hungry wolf. I smile slyly at him as he tries to disregard what he knows he wants. That lip curls as he stalks towards the bed, tugging his tie around his neck.

"Damn you, woman." He climbs across the bed and covers me with his body. Cloaked in fine threads, he presses against me and takes my mouth with such ferocious passion it takes my breath away. His lips crush against mine, desperate and starving. His hand moves to my throat and he lifts my mouth to his, sucking my tongue into his mouth, bruising my lips. My head swirls and I moan into his mouth before he releases me and backs away. "Two can play that game, Beautiful," his sly grin slides into place as he ties his tie, his eyes never leaving mine.

"I have meetings all morning, Sophie. I'll make us a dinner reservation. Charlie will be here for you if you want to go out." He grabs his jacket, kisses me on the forehead and checks his watch. "I hate leaving you, but I have no choice. I will try to wrap up as soon as possible. Maybe we can have lunch, I'll let you know." A quick kiss on the forehead and he saunters out the door.

"Happy Birthday!" I call behind him. He swiftly turns and peaks around the door with the most infectious, pure joy smile.

"Oh, Beautiful. This is already the best birthday yet." And with that he disappears and I sink back under the covers.

***

I spend most of the day prepping, pacing and thinking too much. When I finally get the call from Charlie that he is on his way, I am thankful for the distraction and so nervous. We shared a quiet candle lit dinner in a curved booth, in a smoky corner of an old Italian eatery that felt straight out of Goodfellas. It was romantic and slow, hot and perfect. No bustle of the city or crowds. No schmoozing or networking. Just Rhys and I, tucked in a corner, eyes only for each other. Nothing could have been more perfect, except what I had planned for him when we got home. Everything is set, I made sure before I left. Gifts are in place, the batter is made. Everything is ready, all I need now is the nerve to pull it off. He quietly pays the bill and we slip into the back seat of the car and into city traffic. He takes my face into his hands, our lips meet and electricity fills the car. I am suddenly sure, I can do this.

When we get back to Rhys' place, he retreats to his office for a quick call to his mother and I set to work, still not completely sure this isn't a huge, cheesy mistake. I pull out the waffle iron I bought and take the batter from the refrigerator. It just seemed…right, to make him waffles tonight, for his birthday. Just as I am pulling the first waffle from the iron, he comes strolling into the room, bringing my heart with him.

"Waffles, Beautiful?"

"My version of a birthday cake," I tease, dropping a huge dollop of fresh whipped cream onto his still warm, fresh waffle and pushing it in front of him. His smile is infectious as he takes a seat on a stool and pulls me into his lap.

"Don't make me eat alone." Dipping his finger into the whipped cream, he offers it to me and I gladly take it into my mouth, sucking the whipped cream from the tip of his finger with a playful hum. His eyes glitter in the dull light and that crooked mouth makes my pussy wet. I cannot take much more. But he seems to be enjoying himself, casual, cool, collected and unaffected as he bounces me on his knee, blowing soft breaths across my shoulders. I stand and circle the large island, putting a bit of distance between us, affording myself the ability to think semi-clearly for just a moment. He is like a hypnotist, puts me right down with so little effort.

"What's wrong, Sophie? Why are you all the way over there?" he asks, grinning, knowing full well the answer.

"You are playing with me."

"I love playing with you, Sophie. I could wind you up so tightly." He circles the island coming up behind me, his lips hovering at my ear, his warm breath tickling my neck. "I could make you come without even touching you. Would you like that?"

"Mmm," I purr with my eyes closed, absorbing every last vestige of his adoration and lusty promise.

"I want you to talk to me, Sophie."

"I don't want you to hold back."

"Hmm," he blows across my collarbone. His scent filling my nose as a jolt of electricity courses in my veins. "I do not want to scare you." The threat rolls down my back as he circles me, like a prowling cat.

"I like it," I breathe. "Push me, I need it. I want it." His face lights up at my little request, like a child on Christmas morning, he looks at me with bright, white need.

"Holy hell, Beautiful, Happy Birthday to me!" The words rush out in a heavy whisper, his eyes wide with excitement.

"I got you a gift." I peek at him feeling shy and a little unsure.

"What could be better than waffles? This night just keeps getting better."

Opening a drawer, I pull out a silver box from where I had stashed it away earlier. A momentary hesitation distracts me, thinking about the contents of the box, about what it means now, in the context of last night, and where it may lead. I look up into his eyes and there is no doubt left, evaporated in a moment under his lusty gaze. I hold the box out to him. He cocks his head and takes it, running his finger around the top. Regarding me shrewdly, his fingers tap the top of the box and he smiles. When he pulls the top off, he stops breathing all together, and I am at once embarrassed and excited. Hooking his finger through the metal ring, he holds the handcuffs up, swinging them in front of me.

"Handcuffs?" He is so cute with his crooked grin and his raised brow. A warmth settles over me, making me confident and eager.

"Call it an exercise in trust and commitment. Unzip me," I demand quietly, turning my back to him. This is fun, the illusion of control, the minute amount of power I hold at this moment is utterly intoxicating and sure to be short lived. His fingers run the length of the zipper on my dress, but he never touches me. Every second that he doesn't touch me feels like an eternity. The need for his hands and physicality grows exponentially, he has become a necessity, as have his hands and lips and every other part of him. I hear a small gasp as the zipper slides down my back revealing the lace and bone corset hiding beneath my demure dress. I turn around and slowly let the dress slip from my body, pooling at my feet. His breath catches and he is biting his lip, eyes appraising me like only a he can. I knew the moment I saw it that I had to have it. Lingerie has never been my thing. But with Rhys, I feel like anything can be my thing, if I want it. The delicate, vintage French lace is just the right mix of vixen and goddess. The bones hold me tight, shooting my breasts upward, framing my hips like a burlesque dancer.

"Beautiful," he mouths with heavy breath. Challenge sparkles in his green eyes. "Show me you aren't afraid, Beautiful."

A delicious shiver rolls over my body, culminating in a heavy vibration feeding my belly. My skin prickles at the sight of him with the handcuffs. Biting back a triumphantly crooked grin,

I snatch them from him, quickly slapping one around my wrist. It feels amazing. The bite of the cuff, the coolness of the metal, it all settles between my legs and I am off the charts hot. Looking into Rhys' eyes, I almost shatter on the spot.

"Where do you want me?"

His eyes travel above my head to what I assumed was a pot rack, a wide, metal grid hanging above the island. It is a pot rack, sans pots. Come to think of it, I don't think there has ever been a pot hanging from it as long as I have been here. I guess I never noticed, or just assumed that maybe it was because he doesn't cook. But the sight of it now makes my knees weak. I look back at him and he is watching me intently. His eyes narrow on me and he takes a step forward.

"I have thought about it a few times," he quips with a grin. His excitement is palpable, igniting a slow burn under my skin. I am powerful, and alluring. "One thing is missing," he says to himself. He returns from his room with a silk eye mask. Lifting me to the counter, he commands me to get on my knees. The concrete is smooth and cold against my skin. He easily hops onto the counter and motions for me to put my arms in the air. Winding the loose cuff through the grid, I lift my hand and he closes the cuff tightly around my other wrist. He slides the blindfold over my eyes and hops down from the counter.

With my eyes shrouded in darkness, my other senses spring to life. The sound of my heart pounds in my ears. I am panting, the sound of my shallow breath echoes in my head. My skin prickles with heat. The smell of Rhys' cologne and the faint smell of sweet waffles tickle my nose. And I hear him, watching me. His breathing is shallow and fast.

"Baby, you look amazing." I feel him take a step closer to the counter. With my arms stretched high above me and my knees on the counter, I push my hips in his direction and bow my body towards him. His warm breath swirls in the air, sliding across the tops of my breasts. "I am going to make you come so hard you will lose your breath. You will be dripping wet, Baby. And then I am going to fuck you, and make you come again. You have made my birthday, Beautiful. You have no idea how happy you make me." I feel his lascivious smile and it shoots me into the heavens. I let my head fall back and wait. The heat of his breath and the frantic sound of my own heart are like an erotic tattoo, beating a rhythm that drives me higher and higher. He hasn't even laid a finger on me. Just being strung up like this, shackled in the dark, on display for him, makes me wild with lust. I am pulsing with anticipation.

He is careful not to touch, though I can feel him everywhere, the beat of his heart, the sound of his breath, the smell of his skin. A potent cocktail swirling in the air around me, made all the more intense by my lack of sight. A dozen butterflies take flight in my belly as he hovers in front of me. The ghost of his mouth moves across my jaw and he takes a deep breath. A slight moan sends a chill down my arms as his breath skates across my throat. I bow forward, wanting to feel his warmth.

"Do you want me to touch you?" His voice is smooth like silk.

"Yes," I breathe.

"And, what would you have me do, Sophie?" The sharp edges of the cuffs bite into my wrists as my arms tense and I pull against my restraints. My ears warm and my breasts begin to tingle.

"Kiss me," I breathe, dripping with anticipation and sticky need.

"Here?" His lips hover just out of reach and I pull in the breath he leaves behind. "Here?" His hot breath crosses my shoulder, rippling across the tops of my breasts. My chest heaves in the air, desperate. "How about here?" He blows on my belly, and it ripples across my hips. I writhe with my legs clamped together, hot sticky flesh, grinding into fire, my body climbing higher, chasing more. "Ahhh, here." He blows a steady stream of cool air over my pussy. Although I am covered by a sliver of fine silk tied at both hips, the fabric of my panties is damp making his breath feel cool. I allow my knees to fall open to relieve the fire that burns between my legs. His fingers tug at the tie at my hip and the panties fall away, leaving me bare. He leans closer, hovering in front of me. And as he blows against my clit, I slowly fall over the edge. As if in slow motion, my head falls back in ecstasy, my arms jerk against the cuffs and my heart skips a beat. Holy shit. The darkness allows me to float in quiet bliss. Taking deep breaths letting the aftershocks roll through in slow, fading succession, I fill my lungs with new air and wait. Set adrift so easily, by nothing more than his breath and a few words.

He pulls the blindfold from my eyes and I blink out at him, shocked by the return of the light, dull as it is. We are face to face and I cannot help but grin like a Cheshire cat. He smiles back in triumph, he has yet to touch me. My body cries out at the thought and my hands jerk against the cuffs. Shaking his head slowly, his hands move to my hips, resting lightly over needy flesh. The contact is electric. Our eyes lock and his hands glide over my curves, up over my hips, around my breasts, up my arms and then back down. A shiver runs down my body as his fingers skate the inside of my arms. Leaning in closer, he watches me closely before pressing his lips to my throat. I groan under the weight of his feather light kiss. His hands slide over my breasts and skate across the top of the corset, he dips his finger into the cup and pops my breast out of the lace cage. He places a soft kiss on my sensitive skin before moving his finger to the other side, freeing my other swinging breast. They lay atop their bone cage, forced together pointed and needy. He takes one in his hand and kisses the other. His mouth closes around me, pulling my nipple between his teeth.

"Ah," I moan, propelling him to do the same to the other. Back and forth, kisses and bites, rolling my nipples beneath his tongue, pulling them into his mouth, suckling as if I hold the elixir of life. His other hand glides down my side, settling on my hip. His fingers run along the bottom of the corset, twisting around the clips that hold my stockings, and he smiles against the flesh of my breast. "I love these," he whispers, before tugging it away from my body, letting it snap back against my already sensitive skin. The snap against my thigh stings, ringing in my groin, he snaps the other one, igniting equal fires on either leg before his hands wrap around my thighs. His thumbs draw slow circles around the spot of fire, moving closer and closer to the source of my lust. Pulling my legs further apart, he presses his face into me and takes a deep, appreciative breath, before flicking at my bare flesh with his tongue. His eyes sparkle as he winds one hand around my waist, pulling me closer to him. His mouth moves to the hollow of my throat, but I am distracted by his fingers. They slide slowly into me and then out and he kisses my breath away.

A knock at the door rouses me from a semicoma. I roll over and point my ear to the living room, but cannot find the strength to lift my head from the bed. Overcome by curiosity, I pull on one of Rhys' shirts and pad out of his bedroom into the large loft space. As I come down the stairs, I see Rhys standing with the door half open.

"What are you doing here, Nadja?" I perch at the top of the steps and listen.

"I didn't want you to be alone on your birthday."

"Well, it's not my birthday anymore," he says quietly, glancing up at the grandfather clock that perches just shy of three am, "and I am not alone. It seems you have wasted your time." He looks up the stairs and catches me in his sights, before gracing me with that perfectly crooked, completely relaxed smile.

"What do you mean you are not alone?" She pushes the door open and looks up at me with dark anger clouding her light blue eyes. "What are you doing, Rhys?" She turns to him, then back to me, her face wild with frustration. "What is *she* doing here?"

He looks up at me, a twisted combination of apology and defiance in his eyes before pushing her out the door and following her onto the stoop, pulling the heavy door closed behind them. I hate her. The things she does, the effect she has on him. She makes me feel violent. I turn and head back to the sanctuary of Rhys' oversized bed, curl under the blankets and wait to see which Rhys will return to my side. Will he be tense and agitated, heated?

I must have dozed off because the next thing I know he is sliding in behind me, wrapping me in his strength. His arms a welcome cage, pulling me close, he curls around me and buries his face in my hair.

"Sophie," he whispers. I don't respond, drifting again on the bliss he brought back to bed. "I love…your waffles." I feel the wide girth of his grin as he smiles into my hair. Cheeky devil. I nuzzle against him as he plants a kiss behind my ear and we fall away together, leaving Nadja a distant, fading specter.

Chapter 12

"Happy Birthday, Brother." She stands at the end of my desk with a bottle of my favorite scotch wrapped with a hasty bow.

"This is a lovely surprise." If not predictable, I know she wants something from me. The guise of a birthday gift a perfect in, for whatever it is that she really wants. "My birthday cannot be the only reason for your visit?"

"No, actually, it is Daddy. He wants to have a family weekend in the Hamptons. Will you come?" I look over my computer to see her bright, shining, *I am not telling you everything*, grin. "It has been so long since we have all been together, and Bianca has been asking me about you. It would make them both so happy, Rhys, just come. Two days, that's all."

"I am very busy here. And I have a guest in town, I am not in a position to leave for a few days, I am sorry." I turn my attention back to the computer and hope that she accepts my answer, knowing full well there is a fight on the horizon. She stands there silently, her eyes willing me to meet hers. With a deep sigh of resignation, I give in.

"What is the catch?" I ask, closing my laptop, waiting for the other shoe to drop.

"Well," she trails off, looking out the window, chewing on her lower lip.

"Speak up, please, I don't have all day."

"Nadja is also coming." She steps back and quietly takes a seat before my desk.

"What?"

"Your mother invited her. We ran into her the other day at the Club."

"What were you doing with *her* at the Club?"

"Rhys." She looks at me with those big eyes, begging me to understand. When she knows I never will. "Please, I don't want to go over this, again." She can hardly look me in the eye as she squirms under the well-earned scrutiny she has invited. Yet, as in all things, one can only offer their advice and experience. Everything after that is left to choice and fate. I can no more make this decision for her than I can unmake any of my previous decisions. What is will be, and I know I will not change her mind.

"As long as you are sure, I would never presume to change your mind, I just want to make certain that you are going into this with your eyes wide open. You have seen the havoc and you are assuming the risk, but I won't try and stop you, you know that. So is this what you are here about? Because you know you do not need my approval or permission. But I will not be there." Her silence simmers and I gird myself for a showdown.

"Ok, Rhys, if you don't mind the thought of Bianca and Nadja spending an entire weekend together without you. I'm sure they'll find plenty to talk about." She moves to stand and the thought strikes like lightening. My *mother* and Nadja…alone..in the Hamptons, to plot and scheme. Not a good idea. This cannot happen. The dim flicker of triumph flashes across her face and she sits back down. "Please, Rhys, for me. An entire weekend away with Daddy and Bianca is like torture. They both love it when you are around, take the focus off of me. Please, come. You will make everyone happy."

"You are playing a very precarious game. I am afraid that you are underestimating her and her motives."

"Thanks for the warning, Brother. But I am a big girl and I can handle myself. She cares about me, we have a real connection. Don't begrudge me this, please."

"You are going to have to be honest with everyone eventually, you know. And if you are ashamed of what you are doing, then maybe that is a sign that you shouldn't be doing it."

"Pot, meet kettle," she replies with a smirk. "You should take your own advice," she says, standing. "Next weekend, Brother. Have a happy birthday. I'll call you later." And she sweeps through the door and down the hall before I can tell her no.

***

I walk up the steps and away from the car, a warm breeze blowing across my cheek before the quiet morning is cut by the sound of her shrill purr.

"Sophie." She slithers from the back of a dark car and holds her hand out like she expects me to kiss it or something. I keep my hands firmly at my sides and continue to walk as she falls in beside me. "I don't know what you think you are doing here, but your time is up." Her slimy smile makes my stomach roll. "I thought Rhys had higher standards, but then once a man has been broken, he is never really the same is he?" I stop and look at her. Her eyes hidden behind large sunglasses, her hair perfectly coifed in a high mess on her head. And those full, snide lips that speak such ugly words.

"Rhys is not broken." I answer before I can wish that I hadn't.

"Sure he is, Sweetie." She tips her head in mock sympathy. "You see, I made him and then I broke him and that makes him mine. I got over Rhys a long time ago, but he will *never* be over me. Whatever he is doing with you is purely for my benefit. I am here to remind him that I cannot be replaced and to reclaim my rightful place by his side. A powerful man such as Rhys needs someone who can enrich his life, not a charity case. You are too simple and plain to ever really catch someone like Rhys' attention, can't you see that? He chose you because you were easy, you fulfill some bullshit fantasy that he is sure to tire of. You have let yourself believe the lie and played right into his hand. I was afraid after meeting you in Miami that maybe you had more self-respect than that, but I am glad to know that you wallow down in the gutter with the rest of the sticky trash Rhys happens upon. You are not good enough to be with him. You don't belong here and you don't belong with him. I will make sure of it. Everybody has a breaking point, Sophie. Don't doubt that I will find yours." My nostrils flare and my body begins to tremble with anger, a metallic tang fills my mouth as I bite my tongue. She leans closer and tips her sunglasses down her nose, revealing her bright blue eyes, rimmed with long fake lashes. Chanel Number 5 and cigarette smoke hover around her. "It would be a mistake to underestimate me, Sophie. I am capable of things you could never imagine. Make no mistake, Rhys is mine. And I can do whatever I want with him." She turns and makes her way back down the steps to her waiting car. I look at the street to see Charlie standing at the curb, having witnessed the whole exchange. He doesn't make a move, stays stock still hidden behind black shades, offering no reaction. I take a moment to collect myself. I smooth my clothes and take a deep breath before I step into Rhys' building and watch Kylie emerge from the elevator. What the hell? His exes are suddenly coming out of the woodwork, like cicadas after a long winter they are everywhere and impossible to ignore.

"Sophie!" she squeals, a little too excited, a lot too prepared. "It is so good to see you again. I was just meeting with Rhys and he said you were in town. How do you like the city?"

"I haven't really seen much of it yet. Rhys has been really busy." Her eyes slink between me and the dark car at the curb.

"Well, you must insist that he take you around. Don't let him keep you hidden away.There is so much to see." She turns back towards the car as the door begins to open and she jumps a little, talking faster. "I am sorry, Sophie, you will have to excuse, I, uh, have to get going." She shakes my hands before dashing off towards the waiting car that Nadja has just emerged from. Kylie's eyes dart from me to Nadja before a guilty smile spreads across her dark berry lips and she hurries into the car and out of sight. I watch their car pull into traffic and disappear around a corner. My feet are like old bricks, heavy and on the verge of crumbling to dust. I steady myself with a deep breath and walk into the lion's den. I finger my visitor's badge while I wait for the elevator. What am I going to say when I am finally face to face with him?

Nina is on the phone when I emerge from the elevator and she just waves me past. As I walk down the hallway to Rhys' glass-walled office, my heart skips a beat, the hallway grows longer and everything slows. I watch him as he stands behind his desk, overlooking the city below, a crisp white shirt hangs from his broad shoulders, suspenders crisscross his broad back and hold his pants just perfectly across his high, tight ass. It should be a crime to look that good and be that wholly distracting. I stop and watch him shift his weight from one foot to the other as he rocks his hips back and forth, pacing up and down the wall of windows. He talks as his hands wave above his head, he is animated and agitated when he turns and catches me in his sights. I push through the glass door just as he pulls the Bluetooth from his ear and drops it to his glass desk.

"You are a sight for sore eyes, Beautiful." He saunters over to me and pulls me into an embrace that could melt ice. "You would not believe the morning I have had."

"No? I just ran into Nadja downstairs." His eyes grow wide and he takes a step back. "Oh, and then there was Kylie. Should I expect to run into any other exes today?" He pulls me around his desk and sits in his chair.

"Ok, let's talk." He pulls me into his lap. "First of all, Kylie is not an ex. She is my sister." Shock whips my head around and our eyes meet. "Stepsister is really more accurate. My mother is currently married to her father."

"Oh." I am dumbfounded. Why has he never mentioned this before?

"Nadja must have been with her." He sweeps the hair away from my face and forces our eyes to meet. "They are… friends. Kylie came to discuss some family business. I am sorry that you had to run into her, again." He looks at me with concern in his eyes. "Did you speak to her?"

Do I tell him what just happened? I am afraid to keep bringing her up. Just the mention of her name seems to set him off. And isn't that playing right into her hand, if we are talking about her all the time? If I tell him what she said, he will surely feel the need to confront her, to seek her out. She is wicked and manipulative and the whole situation sets my pulse racing uncomfortably.

"Um, no. No, we didn't speak." I will not give her the satisfaction. I can handle myself. If she thought I was going to run to Rhys, she has underestimated me.

We spend a couple of leisurely hours together. We stroll through Central Park, have a hot dog for lunch, watch the boaters. I could be walking through a dozen movies. He reminds me that we are having dinner with Olivia and Matthew as they have finally returned, and I am more than grateful for the distraction from Nadja, for a familiar, friendly face. I can't wait to see Olivia. I have missed her more than ever before. When my phone beeps for the fourth time, I can no longer ignore what I have pushed to the back. I have emails piling up, communications from the estate lawyer. I have to check back in to my own life.

"I need to get back to the office, Beautiful, just for an hour or so. Will you be alright?" he asks as we walk over the small stone bridge back towards the edge of the Park. "Charlie will take you home and I'll meet you there shortly, okay?" The way he so casually calls it "home", as if it's *my* home too, makes me suddenly so aware of our precarious situation. "Hello? Earth to Sophie." I am shaken from my imagined struggle and look into his big green eyes and find nothing but warmth. I don't need to worry. Right? We are great, things are going well. I smile brightly as he kisses me on the corner of my mouth and pulls me towards Charlie and the waiting car.

"I need to check a few emails, Rhys, can I use your computer?" I ask as we pull to the curb at his office building.

"Of course you can, Beautiful. My laptop should be in the bedroom, help yourself and I will see you shortly." He kisses me like a long hard goodbye before leaving me with a low grumble and a wink.

Chapter 13

As Charlie and I lurch through traffic, my mind wanders to the situation I have really created here. I am getting swallowed by his life so easily, so quickly. Maintaining balance is key and he throws me off kilter. If things don't work out, I am on my own, I need to be in control. To drive my life. I cannot be absorbed into his world. I will surely lose myself and become my nightmare and his *former*. How long can this work before the curtain is ripped back, exposing me for a fraud, for a hypocrite, engulfed in artificial bliss and sexual heroin? The bile rises in my throat at the thought, and at how quickly my mind spins out of control. I tap the keyboard to wake the computer that Rhys so graciously donated in hopes of distracting myself. The screen springs to life with a black and white photo, large and strikingly focused, the tight curve and dramatic shadow of a woman's hip sways across the screen, a cross section of dark and light. Folders pop up around the perimeter of the screen, and a window opens with what looks like Rhys' email. I do not want to read his email. But, damn if her name doesn't just jump off the screen and stab me in the heart when I think of the lengths I have gone to, to convince Rhys, and myself, that I am not wildly insecure about her. It is a lie, as I stare at her name in his inbox, I hate her, there needs to be a new word for hate, I loathe her. I do not want to read whatever melodious bile she writes to Rhys, rehashing the past or desperately clinging to him out of spite. My hands hover over the keyboard. I move the cursor to close the window, banish her from the screen, when I hear Rhys.

"Where are you, Beautiful? I am a starving man, come feed me, woman!" Pleasure licks at my spine, and I close my eyes to absorb every last drop. He walks into the room and I melt a little. Bending down over me, he gives me a long, soft kiss, running his tongue along my lips, ringing in my head like a bell choir.

"I was just going to check my email when an email popped up for you from Nadja." I push the laptop towards him and hop from the bed heading to the bathroom to give him privacy. He plops down on the bed and pulls the computer into his lap.

"Did you read these?" he calls, a slight edge in his tone.

"No way, I wouldn't do that. Why? What does she want?" I walk back into the room and stare into his dark, hollow eyes. I want to know why she is emailing him, what she is saying. But I don't want him to know that, I don't really want to admit it to myself. The color has drained from his face.

"To drive you away," he murmurs, barely audible.

"Well, she can't." I sidle up behind him and wrap my arms around his neck. Looking down into his inbox there are several messages from her now, all labeled with similar titles, RNM, RNC, RNH, NSR, RNZ, RNDC, RNKA, NWR, nine in all. What the fuck is she doing? "You want me here, right?" I tease, squeezing him closer to me, tamping down the ever growing knot of jealousy that is settling in my belly.

"Yes, more than anything," he rushes, the panic palpable now.

"Well then, she can't possibly hurt us. Just open it, see what she has to say." I reach down and double tap the cursor.

"Wait, Sophie! No!" But it is too late, my fingers have done the damage. I feel the color run from my face as a grainy video pops up. Staring back at me is a woman with a ball in her mouth, held too tightly by a menacing leather strap, hovering on all fours. Another woman dressed in stockings and heels towers behind her and hits her, hard, with a long riding crop. A man's well shaped legs enter the shot and he moves behind her. She is panting, excited even, her face alight with anticipation. Melissa. Her dark eyes sparkle with that ego I saw in Miami as she stares into the camera, waiting. My stomach drops to the floor and my eyes are wide with fear for her, for me, as he moves to his knees behind her and fixes to slide his impressive cock into her quivering body. He sinks into her, lifts his head and looks dead at the camera. I am staring into eyes that make my heart stop. Everything comes crashing down. *Damn it! I wish I had never seen that, I did not want to see that.* I take a deep breath and hope for steady, but it does not come easy. I do not know what to do with this information. It is playing on a loop, stuck behind my eyes, and Rhys just watches me. I think I'm going to be sick. I push away from him and jump from the bed, ready to strike.

He sits, stone still, silent and pale as a ghost. I stand and watch him for what feels like forever. I watch him, like watching a monkey at the zoo. Waiting for them to screech, or make a face, or move. Dance monkey! But he remains a stone. I cannot even tell if he is breathing he is so stiff, he is motionless, and seemingly emotionless.

"Say something, Rhys." I shiver at the quiet menace in my own voice. "Say something before my mind runs away." My voice gets softer and softer as my blood pounds louder in my ears. I do not have the tools to deal with this, I do not even know how I feel. I feel sick, but surely that is because of Nadja. Everything she does makes me feel nuts, did she do this on purpose? Of course she did! She warned me not to underestimate her. And that was Melissa. What the hell? Everything about her makes more sense, she warned me too. No wonder she was such a bitch. I look up to find a still silent Rhys, gripping the now closed laptop with white knuckles, all the color drained from his face. Fuck.

"Sophie." His voice crackles with pain when he finally finds his voice and I almost feel bad for him. But in that moment, when his lips move around my name, all I feel is white hot anger. He is a snake charmer and I am a fool. Every twist and turn has an excuse, and every time I accept whatever it may be. Charmed by his snake, his magic, I forget myself. He steps to the middle of the room and I move to get around him, knowing I have little capacity to withstand his touch. I back away from him and watch the gravity of the situation move across his eyes, a shadow of disbelief, and blooming frustration.

"Please! Don't." It starts as a booming yell, but ends in a whimper. I cannot rectify what I just saw, cannot shake it off. I back away from him.

"Sophie." His tone is quiet, addressing a frightened babe. "I am sorry that you had to see that. I am sorry about everything. But, please. Let me explain. I told you she was trying to drive you way." I shake my head violently, knowing that he will spin it all and I am clearly so foolish when it comes to him, so blind. I am unwilling to hear anything. I cannot bear the sound of his voice. I shake my head.

"She knew what she was doing, Sophie. Please don't let her win. What you saw is my past. That is from almost two years ago, Sophie."

"Shhhh!" I hiss at him. "Please, stop." My ears burn, when I close my eyes my mind burns. There is no escape, no going back. Gripping my arms, he pulls me closer, winding his hand around my neck, immobilizing me with just his hand, forcing me to look into those eyes. "Of course she knew. She warned me."

"What do you mean she *warned* you? What are you talking about, Sophie? You said that you didn't speak with her."

"Well, I did OK! I didn't want to give her the satisfaction of your attention. I didn't want her to ruin our day, so much for that!" I back away from him, out of his reach.

"I don't want this, Sophie. Not like this."

"Please. Don't touch me like that, not now. I can't take it." I push against his stone chest, knowing it could kill me. His strong hand wound about my neck, cradling my head, I will surely melt, or break. My heart is being strangled, squeezed within an inch of life. I can hardly catch my breath or stand still. Tears well in my eyes, I am drowning from within. A sob so deep it climbs from my toes threatens the cool silence between us, but I bite it back, a small bead of blood growing inside my bottom lip. I push past him and walk from the room with him just at my heels.

"Please, don't leave." He grabs his keys from the counter quickly snapping them into his palm. "Please don't leave," he insists, "I will go. I will give you space, but please don't leave." I just shake my head at him, barely holding it together, my arms wrapped so tightly across my chest. He backs into the hallway and pleads again, a last ditch whisper. "Please, don't leave." I close the door on Rhys' fallen face and the man who knows me best, the man I thought I knew. My heart is shattered, my legs no longer able to support the weight I have thrust upon them. My heavy, wounded heart pushes me down, I slide against the door, holding my back rigid, the floor stopping me from sinking into oblivion. The growing sob lodged in my throat finally escapes, ripping a hole in my heart, releasing the flood gates, welcoming the dark.

***

A loud sob erupts from her chest the moment she closes the door and I am a pillar, trapped on the spot, unable to walk away from her when she is in such pain. Like an immovable stone, I stand on the other side of the door and listen to her sink to the floor and cry. Her pain is palpable, filling the hallway, threatening to swallow me, as it should. I am the cause of her immense pain, I am the cause, again. I sit with my back to the door, my back to hers, and wait. For never ending moments, pain filled sobs are torn from her chest, full of heavy sorrow. I have never heard a more painful sound in my life. Finally, her cries grow softer as she catches her breath and I am grateful for her steady breathing, her fading sobs. She lets out a small groan, as if reminded of what she saw. Damn it! OK, so she saw me fucking Melissa while Nadja watched. A pit of growing anger settles in my gut and my blood begins to churn with questions, and an ever evolving anger. Struck by how reckless Nadja has become, she would risk exposing herself just to keep me from being happy. Sophie's cries stop and I press my ear to the door, trying to hear her move. A hollow thud catches my attention as her shadow moves under the door.

"Sophie? Are you OK?" I hear her shuffle and her shadow disappears. A hysterical chuckle rattles from her throat and I can tell that she is still fighting tears.

"Rhys, what are you doing?" Her voice is raw and broken.

"I didn't want to leave you." She shifts and I turn and press my ear to the door. Her heart tugs at me across the barrier that divides us while I listen to her breathe, growing steady and deep, weaved with a quiet whimper. When her breath catches, her waves of grief wrap around my heart threatening to strangle me, squeezing the life out of me for hurting her.

"I'm glad you're still here," her hushed voice rings like a choir on high.

"I will never walk away from you, Sophie." Her long silence slices through me.

"I don't know what to do."

"Ok. I will sit here all day, Beautiful. Whatever you want, whatever you need. I am just so deeply sorry that you had to see that." And I am, with every cell in my body. I wish I could take it back, but it cannot be erased or avoided.

"I am sorry, too." After a long pause, an uncomfortable question crosses the door. "Are there more?" Her voice is barely audible, but echoes in my head. There is more, so much more. Fear grows like a beast and erupts from my chest in a fit of regretful disclosures.

"Sophie. I have done a lot of stupid things. It was a different time, I was a different person. Things were just, different. I don't know what I can say." And I have no idea what I want him to say. How do you explain that away? "I know that you probably don't understand, but I beg of you to hear me out. I was a jerk. I have always been in control, always gotten what I wanted. And after a while that sort of spoiled indulgence makes you dark and jaded. But, with you, I have no control. The closer I get to you, the deeper I push the less control I have. I can't remember any of those girls. Not their faces, not their names. Not since you. You wiped it all away. There is only you. You are my saving grace."

"Do you still want that?"

"No! My God, Sophie. It is all in the past, where it should have stayed. She is just trying to drive you away."

"Good." I hear her whisper. After a long pause, she breaks the silence. "Have you ever filmed me?"

"No!" The strangled declaration rips from my throat. "Sophie, I would never do that to you."

"Why did you do it?" The small whisper shrouds the force of a harsh question. How am I supposed to answer that? We were young, jaded and utterly bored. Everything was done to the extreme, so much experimenting and debauchery. I don't know how to answer. I fill my lungs and try to form an answer that makes sense, that will satisfy her, without hurting her.

"I was a jerk, Sophie. It's in a man's best interest to hide the worst parts of himself. I never wanted you to know those parts."

"You can't pick and choose, Rhys. If we are going to be together, I need to know all your parts." I smile to myself, knowing she is right and elated at her admission that we are together.

"Are we together?" I ask with undisguised hope.

"Rhys, I am here aren't I? I have locked myself in *your* apartment. I am not going anywhere, unless you continue to keep me in the dark. You cannot hide who you were. It makes you who you are. I hate what I saw. I hate that you did any of it. But what you did back then has nothing to do with me, right?"

"I didn't mean to keep you in the dark. I thought I was protecting you." The lock slides open and she stands above me. I move to my feet, backing away from the door. Her shoulders slump forward and she expels a deep, long held breath. Allowing a small smile to raise the corner of her tear stained mouth, she shakes her head and I am lost. Stepping into the hallway, she takes me by surprise when she takes my hand and pulls me back into the apartment. Squeezing my fingers as she kicks the door shut, I am hopeful.

"I don't need your protection, Rhys, I just need you." Her wide green eyes are red rimmed, glossy with fading tears, and I am trapped. Even as her face is stained with tears, she is beautiful, and she needs me. "You need me?" I relish in the thought. She scoffs at the question, wrinkling her eyebrow.

"Yes. You have become something of a necessity. Are you happy?"

"You have no idea." I am elated, beyond my wildest dreams. She needs me. The thought soothes my soul, a welcome cloak of contentment wrapped around my shoulders. She will be my light as I fight off the dark.

We stand in the entryway, bathed in the fading rays of the sun. I feel like I am holding on for dear life, grasping at something that could fall away at any moment. Yet he stands here, steadfast in my arms.

"What did she say to you, Sophie?" He holds me at arms-length at watches my face twist with remembrance.

"Nadja? She seems to think that you have not outgrown her." His eyes narrow in on me. "She laughed in my face. Told me that you were broken, that she broke you." His icy reaction chills my blood. "She said that I wasn't good enough for you. That everyone had a breaking point. She warned me not to underestimate her." Nostrils flaring like a bull, he rubs his hands up my arms, pulls me closer and waits. Towering above me, he waits for me to close the gap and curl into him, and I want to. But my feet will not allow it, his hands on my arms, the feel of his skin against mine, looking him in the eyes burns, bringing flashes of the grainy video. I want to claw my eyes out. Tears well up and I start to sob. "God, it hurts." I grasp at the sucking wound in my chest. "I wish I had never seen it." His face twists in pain while he watches me suffer. "Every time I close my eyes, there you are." A shiver rolls through me and my whole body shakes uncontrollably.

"We will have to replace what is behind those lids. I think I can do that." The edge is still sharp, but his voice is warm and silky, yet rubs me the wrong way. This is not a joke. My mind is permanently seared with a vision that I cannot escape.

"How would you feel if you saw a video of me like that?" I snap at him.

"Am I in the video?" he smirks. His mistimed teasing may cost us both if he doesn't take this seriously.

"Do I seem in a joking mood?"

"No, sorry." He steps back and looks at me, searching my face.

"Rhys, you almost lost your mind over some guy I used to know for like a minute, five years ago. There is no video, no evidence and certainly no extensive digital library of my past escapades. How would you feel if you saw me and Andrew?" His eyes grow dark, his form more rigid and I know he is thinking about it, thinking about me, on my knees with some strange man kneeling behind me. He looks into my eyes and I see the ice form across his once warm, green pools.

"Murderous," he growls through gritted teeth

"Exactly!" Finally, he understands!

"Well, we can't kill Nadja." His tightly wound voice struggles to sound light and jovial. I step closer to him and gingerly curl against his chest.

"Oh, I don't want to kill her. I want to hurt her." Listening to his rapid heart and ragged breath, I am overcome, wading in hatred. Never has another person solicited such violent feelings of hate. Running my hands down Rhys' back, I think about what she has tried to do, over and over again and I hate her. She keeps trying to take this away from me. I will not let her.

"Are we ok?" he asks.

"We will be." And I mean it. I am not okay now, but I will be.

"Still up for dinner tonight? Olivia called and was not in a flexible state of mind, she is missing you. But, if you're not up to it…"

"That sounds fine. I just need a little time, an hour or so." His brows knit together and he questions me with his eyes, looking down at his watch.

"OK, Beautiful. I can give you an hour. I have a quick errand to run and then I will pick you up. How does that sound, Beautiful?" It stings a bit when he says it, and I know what I have to do.

"Yes, that sounds perfect." And as much as I want him to stay, I want him to go. I need some time to process, and plan. I need to scrub my body and face of the filth that Nadja continues to hurl at me. Tipping my head to meet his eyes, he kisses me lightly at the corner of my mouth and turns on his heel. As he swings the door open, he winks at me with his crooked grin solidly in place.

"I'll be back in a little while, Sophie. Be ready."

Chapter 14

I am waiting at the curb when Rhys and Charlie return, ready to see Olivia, needing the company of others, a buffer of sorts. We ride in relative silence, Rhys feels pensive but grins at me and holds my hand tightly.

Olivia and Matthew are waiting when we arrive and I am so excited to see her, a familiar face, someone I understand. I am overwhelmed and know immediately that the night will not be easy. She reads me like a book and immediately asks what is wrong as soon as she embraces me.

"Nothing." I shake her off taking my seat next to Rhys. She watches shrewdly as we order drinks and Rhys pulls a brown leather box from his coat pocket. Her eyes grow wide with excitement as he places it in front of me.

"I got you a little something today, Sophie."

"Rhys, you shouldn't have. Why did you do this?" I ask, genuinely curious and more than a little taken aback. He takes the cover off the box to reveal a beautiful, sparkling rose gold watch, the face surrounded by dazzling diamonds that twinkle like little stars. Olivia's eyes dart to her own wrist, as she scrutinizes both watches, needing hers to be better.

"Wow," she huffs, pulling the watch closer to her face.

"Rhys." I am speechless. The watch sparkles in the flickering candlelight of the table, facets fire and bounce from Olivia's wide eyes to Rhys' waiting face.

"Do you like it?" he asks, taking the box from my hand. He takes the watch from the pillow and holds it out to me. I offer him my wrist with not a word hanging from my mouth.

"You guys must be serious," Olivia muses, still unable to take her eyes off the watch that Rhys has now placed around my wrist. It is colder and heavier than it looks, but it feels nice. His eyebrows hang high on his face as he waits with baited breath for my reaction. I have never received such an extravagant present. I have never owned anything so beautiful. And I have never wanted to take a piece of jewelry off so badly in all of my life. Suddenly, it feels like an anchor around my wrist, a cold metal anchor, tugging me to the ground. I slip the watch off my wrist and quickly tuck it back around its pillow and into the box. Rhys' face falls for a moment.

"I love it, really." *It's way too much.*

"It's time," he offers quietly, sliding his hands across the table, covering my fingers with his. "You said you needed time. So I am giving you *time*." He grins and it twists in my gut. God, he is so beautiful. How did this happen? I struggle to remember how I got here, with him. This person who is so far out of my league, everyone around him can see it. He is blind to it. How long until he changes his mind, or gets bored, until the need to be pushed comes back. How do I move past these damn pictures in my head of him and Melissa and Nadja? If I could just erase it, I know I could move on, I want to just move on. The past is in the past, I would prefer to leave both of our pasts behind us.

"Time? Why do you need time?" Olivia asks, sipping her white wine, sticking her nose where it doesn't belong. I look into Rhys' eyes for some guidance. What am I supposed to say? He is the one who brought it up. But before I can respond, Rhys turns to Matthew.

"Nadja is on the war path and has painted a target on Sophie's back." Matthew's eyes light up with humor before he looks at me with pity. "She is in the mood to spill secrets, so I had to tell Sophie the truth."

Matthew squirms slightly, but it is Olivia's reaction that catches my attention. A breath catches in her throat and she coughs violently, before grasping my arm.

"About time," she mutters, trying to catch her breath. Matthew looks down at her, but her eyes flash back in warning. "What truth?"

"Babe," Matthew warns.

"No, Matthew. Sophie is *my* friend, and if we hadn't been half way around the world and I had known this was going on and he *still* hasn't told her *the truth* I would have told her myself. You need to tell her everything, Rhys, like now." My heart races at her candor and force. She waits impatiently, looking from Matthew to Rhys. "In my experience, it is best to just rip the bandage off, wouldn't you say, guys? Just spill it and let it be over." Her eyes bore a hole through Rhys, but he says nothing, his white-knuckle grip on his glass the only indication that he is in fact not made of stone.

Olivia grabs my hand, "You know what? We are going to the bar!" She pulls me behind her. "I will rip the damn bandage myself." We wind through the crowd and slide into the last two empty bar stools. I look back at the table to see Rhys watching me, swirling his scotch the way he does when he is anxious.

"What do you know?" Olivia demands as she motions to the bartender. Two shots of whiskey slide down our throats before I can loosen my tongue enough to talk. A huge part of me does not want to tell her anything, does not want to talk about it. But, clearly she knows something. She must, the way she and Matthew are acting. I tell her about running into Andrew and that distracts her momentarily. "Oh, my God! Yes, Andrew. I remember you telling me about him, that Australian rugby player?" She shivers and blows a mock breath. "He was hot! How did that go?" she asks, tossing back another shot of Jack.

"Not well. Rhys was mad with jealousy and we went through this whole power struggle thing." I toss back my shot and continue on, my tongue thoroughly loose and my mind now reeling with so many details. "I got pissed at the way he acted, like I was his property or something." Olivia's eyebrows go up, but not in surprise. "He wanted to be the only guy, he said. Isn't that bullshit? Here he is with this supermodel ex, not to mention the fact that he apparently slept with half the women at your wedding! And now, he is throwing a fit about me seeing some guy I hooked up with years ago, before I even knew him?" Another round of shots land in front of us, I slam mine back and continue. "And Nadja! Don't get me started on that bitch!"

The music is getting louder as the crowd grows and we are pressed to the bar by the throngs of people. Jack flows through me like life blood and I cannot stop talking, it is cathartic to lay all this shit out. Olivia is clearly in a listening mood, hanging on my every word, words that become looser and juicier with every shot. "She showed up at his house on his birthday, correction, at three am the morning *after* his birthday. When he told her he was not alone, girl, I thought her head was going to explode. But when she saw me, there was a fire in her eyes like I have never seen."

"She is crazy!" Olivia yells over the crowd.

"This morning she accosted me on the front steps of Rhys' office building."

"Oh, my God! What did she say? What happened?"

"She basically threatened me. Said I wasn't good enough, and that Rhys will never outgrow her. She told me not to underestimate her." We toss back another shot.

"What did you do?" Olivia yells, leaning in closer. "What did Rhys say?"
I lean back and look into her face. A weird light flashes across her eyes like she knows, and suddenly I feel sick. If she knows, then Matthew knows. Again, I am the only one in the dark.

"Why didn't you tell me Kylie was Rhys'stepsister?" I ask, distracted by my own clashing inner monologues. Her eyes grow wide and she shakes her head in confusion. Wait, she said, *in my experience.* A pang of anger twists in my belly, radiating into the rest of my body. I tilt my head at her in question.

"You said 'in your experience' what did that mean? What do *you* know, Olivia?" I ask as the music softens. She reaches across the bar and grabs the last shot. "Was Matthew with Nadja, too?"

"What? No!" she declares. "That bitch is a special kind of crazy that only Rhys could appreciate. Fuck it!" she says, pouring the last shot into her mouth. "Rhys and Matthew used to go to these…clubs. Bondage clubs, sex clubs, they pretty much made the circuit." I shake my head in disbelief, this is *not* what we were talking about. But, I listen in fascination as the whiskey has caused an avalanche of information to come dislodged and I want to catch it all. "Apparently they had quite the reputation, girls would throw themselves at them, let them do whatever they liked. I know the two of them have shared girls. *That* was a hard one to swallow. Then they started hosting *Private Parties*," she mutters, mostly to herself. "What happened exactly?"

"She sent Rhys these emails, videos. I mean, I think they were all videos. We only opened one." She waits sternly, motioning to the bartender one more time. I lower my voice and lean closer to her. "It was Melissa, he and Nadja were fucking Melissa. She was gagged, and…." My stomach lurches into my throat and I stop talking, close my mouth and wish it all weren't true. Sitting back on my stool, I fill my lungs with a deep breath of the stagnant bar air. "He didn't say a word about a club or parties. He just told me about his relationship with Nadja. He said they pushed each other. That they weren't good for each other."

"You got that right!" she says, slapping the bar as two more shots of whiskey are poured. "He and Nadja are like poison to each other. But, his sins are his own." We toast with what I hope is the last round of shots.

"I don't know what to do." My voice is soft after hacking and coughing. The last shot burning on the way down. Sliding through my body like the swell of information, licking my veins, clouding my reason.

"My first *Private Party* was Matthew's last, needless to say. Nadja and Rhys continued until she disappeared, which was and always has been her pattern. God only knows what kind of shit those two got up to. Sophie, these people are another breed, seriously. Some of the things I have seen would blow your mind. When we were playing spin the bottle in my basement with stolen wine coolers, they were hosting gold plated orgies on their parent's yacht in the south of France.

"And you're ok with that?"

"I have to be. I mean, I am now, I wasn't at first, I was jealous and angry and…disgusted. It took some getting used to. But that is in the past. Matthew loves me and I love him. So, Rhys made a little video," she says a little too loudly, and in the blink of an eye she is more than a little drunk. "That is all in Rhys' past, I am sure of it. Everybody has a past. What matters is how you feel. Matthew and I have our own demons. We have worked them out and I have moved on." Her eyes are wide when she leans in and kisses me on the cheek.

"Sophie. You have to decide if you can accept this or not. Rhys has grown, he isn't the same person that he was with Nadja. We have never seen him this way. Matthew says has never seen Rhys this happy, ever. Not with Nadja. I know he has been trying to turn things around. But you have to decide if you believe it, and if you can live with it, because if you can't let it go it will haunt you every day." She slides forward on her stool and stumbles to her feet. I wrap my arms around her and steady her. "Whoa!" she yells, throwing her arms around my shoulders. "No more Jack for me, girl!"

"Yeah, me either." Another drink would surely push me off the deep end. "Come, let's go back to the table. The boys are watching us." Rhys quickly pays the check as we approach the table and they shuffle us out to the curb before we can sit.

Chapter 15

"Matthew, it was good to see you, Brother. Good luck with her," Rhys teases, shaking Matthew's hand.

"It looks like you need the luck tonight, my friend. We'll talk on Monday." He pats Rhys on the shoulder and walks around his car to meet the valet.

"Bye, Sophie!" Olivia throws her loose arms around my neck and gives me a squeeze that pushes me off balance. We both sway and fall from the curb, stumbling over our shoes, giggling in each other arms. Rhys pulls us back from the street and hands Olivia off to Matthew before pushing me into the back of his Town Car. A loud giggle erupts from my throat as I slide across the seat watching Rhys' dark face focus on me. I am drunk, the whiskey having caught me, and I don't care. Jack slows the blood in my veins, wrapping me in a veil of alcohol infused indifference. He sits back, staring at me and I find it impossible to take him seriously.

"You are angry," I whisper.

"You are drunk," he states with no emotion.

"You have no right to be angry with me," I retort. He softens with a sigh.

"I am not angry, Sophie. I am worried." The car weaves through traffic, speed ebbing and flowing, throwing my gut into a tailspin, stop lights and street lights cast shadows that make the car spin and I need fresh air. I scoot to the corner and roll the window down. Resting my head against the seat, I let my eyes close and it all comes back into focus. Melissa's blazing eyes stare at me from behind my lids, her smile wide and triumphant as she takes everything that Rhys can give. Damn Her! I sit straight up my eyes wide, my throat on fire.

"You should be worried. What am I supposed to think? How am I supposed to handle this?" Quiet words start to fall like rain, an inner monologue going public. I work through it out loud as if Rhys isn't even there. "You have not been honest. You have been withholding vital information about yourself, Mr. Slate. I mean, guys like you are so used to everything just falling at your feet. Of course, women would fall at your feet. Hell, I fell at your feet against my better judgment. But bondage clubs and *private parties*? Really? I know what that means! Orgies! I knew you were no saint, but this is a whole other level. I have been with five people. Five! And I thought I was skating the lines of impropriety. I shudder to think how many women, how many girls you have been with. Just the thought makes me want to vomit. And the video! Ugh! The video has been playing on a loop in my mind, over and over again. How am I supposed to get rid of that?" I let my head fall back against the seat and look anywhere but into his eyes. "What the hell have I gotten myself into? How is it possible that you will not get bored with me and drop me so fast my head spins? Why would *you…*" My arm flies across the car in a grand gesture, waving about his form. "You! Why would you be interested in me? What happens when I don't want to do the things you like? What if I can't handle you? What if I'm not enough?" I sit back against the seat and take a deep breath of the warm summer air that flows through the window. "I just ran away, again. I ran away from my problems and into the arms of a man." I watch him now, across the car his eyes sparkle in the dark, but he says nothing. "You will crush me, Rhys. I will get lost in you and I will never recover. That is a scary thought. But it is even scarier to think of my life without you. How did you do that?" I close my eyes and rest, willing my stomach to settle, willing the whiskey to wear off, yet I know it is only going to get worse before it gets better. "You should be worried."

The next thing I know Rhys is setting me down on the bed and pulling off my shoes. I sit up and look into the eyes of a worried soul. His features are twisted and pulled down in a sad frown, lines dart across his forehead and his eyes are black.

"I think I'm a little drunk," I whisper, letting my head fall back as he climbs up next to me.

"Just a little," he murmurs with a chuckle, propping himself on his elbow to look at me.

"I think maybe I should go home for a little while." I roll into a ball facing him. His eyes flash, his tight jaw saws back and forth before his eyebrows knit together.

"Why?" A drunken jumble of reasons swims through the muck of my head, but I can't come up with one good cohesive stream of consciousness.

"You know why, Rhys. I just need a little time, maybe a little distance." His face wrinkles and he opens his mouth to respond before snapping it shut. "I don't think straight when it comes to you." He just watches me trying to work it all out. He reaches out and brushes a hair from my forehead.

"I have the same problem," he mutters before kissing my forehead.

"Really?" I don't believe it. I know he says it, but men say what they need to say, to get what they want.

"More than you can know, Sophie. You are so much more than I deserve." The room starts to slowly spin as I take a deep breath and sit up, Rhys follows. "Are you alright?" His hand on my knee settles me and I close my eyes to stop the spin. "You need water. I will be right back." He slides off the bed and disappears. I take the moment to try and gather myself.

I go into the bathroom and smooth my clothes, splash a little water on my face and brush my teeth. The taste of whiskey coats my mouth, leaving a regretful film that tortures me. Rhys hands me a tall glass of water as I step back into the room. His tall, lean body looms large and he hovers, waiting for what, I don't know, for me to throw up, pass out, or run, either way, he looks like he is anticipating something very unpleasant. I reach up and cup his cheek. His warm skin feels nice on my palm, a little rough from his stubble.

"Don't look so sad." He grabs my hand and places a slow, soft kiss to my palm. Closing his eyes, he rests my palm against his lips and takes a deep breath.

"Please, don't leave me, Sophie." His coal black eyes pull at my heartstrings.

"I am not leaving you, Rhys." I stretch on my tip toes and kiss the corner of his mouth. He sweeps me up into his arms, flush against his chest, knocking the almost empty glass from my hand. It bounces and skids to the foot of the bed, leaving a small puddle in its wake, but Rhys doesn't seem to care. He walks to the bed, kicking the glass out of the way as he lowers me onto the mattress. The kiss is all consuming, our breaths mingled and dancing over our teeth as lips press and twist around each other. Our tongues swirl around and around, pushing in and out. His teeth graze my bottom lip and he nips me quickly.

"What did Olivia say to you?"

"She said the past is in the past, I just have to decide if I can live with it."

"And can you?"

"I don't really have a choice, do I?"

"I am sorry, Sophie."

"I don't want you to be sorry, Rhys. Truly, it shouldn't matter. It has nothing to do with me, I know that. It is in the past. I have a past. We have been over this. I can handle that. But I cannot forget what I saw. Every time I close my eyes, I see her face, I see you. It is burned into my mind, and it hurts like a fucking wound." We lay face to face and silent for a long moment, a stretched moment of silence that seemed perfect.

"Rip it off," I whisper, "just tell me everything. That way she has no power over you anymore. No power over us. I want to understand. I promise I will try." His brow furrows in thought and he shakes his head in frustration.

"I don't want to lose you, Sophie."

"Just tell me so we can move on."

"Well, alright." He hops from the bed. "I guess if we are going to do this I should have a drink, maybe a few so I can catch up to you." I tip my head at him and gesture for my own glass.

"I am deeply flawed, Sophie. And you, you are so not." I snort in indignation as we toss back our whiskey in unison, eyeing each other in challenge.

"No flaws! Are you serious? I am twenty four years old and I am afraid of everything. I live my life like I am eighty. I stayed with a man that hurt me just because I was afraid to be alone. There are your flaws, and that's just a scratch at the surface."

"You have good reason behind your bad decisions, Sophie. I have nothing of substance. No good excuse. I was simply young and bored. There is no excuse for that. No silver lining that will redeem me." He paces at the foot of the bed, like a caged animal. "I really don't want to do this. You realize what you are asking me to do right? You are asking me to expose myself, to rip back the mask and show you the guy I have worked so hard to hide. I like to bury my flaws deep, Sophie. Willingly bringing them into the open is counterintuitive. It is in every man's best interest to present his best self. You are asking me to willingly show you the monster that lurks beneath. What if you decide you don't like what you see? I don't want to lose you, Sophie. You are asking me to take a big risk here."

"And you have asked me to take a risk. I am here, Rhys. I took a risk for you, you have to trust me."

"I know you are right. So, go ahead, ask me anything."

"Oh no, I want you to just tell me. No loop holes in case I don't ask the right questions, no escape, Rhys. If you want me to trust you, you have to be honest with me. I cannot keep being bombarded by your past. I don't know how much more I can take. You have to let me in."

"What are the chances you are going to remember any of this anyhow?"

"Slim to none," I tease as the room tilts on its axis and a drunken fog fills my head.

"Matthew and I were wild in our younger days. There were...*girls*. We went to clubs, fetish clubs and we would pick up someone to play with. Nothing everyone else wasn't doing. Sometimes we would play with people we knew. I would bring Nadja when she was in town, and she got really into it. It was exhilarating, the power play, the submission. The things girls were willing to do just to be near us, just to party on our boat. It's hard not to let that kind of attention and access go to your head when you are a young man. We started to make a name for ourselves so we had to take it underground. We started hosting the Private Parties Olivia told you about. But once Matthew and Olivia got serious, he didn't like to play anymore. It was just me and Nadja. Nadja loves to perform for the camera so we started to tape it. It became a *thing*, women would vie for her attention when we were out just for a chance to hook up with us." I wince at the thought of them hooking up with a group.

"Like two addicts, we just fed off of each other's compulsion to push. We were always pushing each other, sometimes to uncomfortable heights. It was so easy to get carried away and Nadja loves to exploit other people's weaknesses. She gets off on humiliation and exploitation. It was mesmerizing the things that she could get people to do, with so little effort. But she took it too far. She tried to *bring me a girl*, one night in Ibiza, a real piece of work that she had clearly already worked over, some piece of Eurotrash that she had a grudge against. She tried convincing me that we should use her and document it so Nadja could humiliate her. She was so cold about it, so devious and I just didn't want any part of it. We had already crossed so many lines, but I had finally found the line I wouldn't cross. I saw Nadja in a whole new light, it was like having the curtain ripped back, revealing the great and powerful Oz to be a fraud. Nothing more than a face, a façade, perfect on the outside, but nothing at the core. I realized that I had to get away from her. We had gone back and forth for years, suddenly I just couldn't remember why. She left for a job and I never looked back. I threw myself back into work and went back to business as usual. We didn't see one another or speak for almost six months." He takes a deep breath before continuing.

"But you have to understand, because our relationship was always so back and forth, she traveled so much and really wasn't around. So leaving her behind was something I was more than prepared to do. We ran into each other at a charity event, which was bound to happen. I wasn't sure what to expect, but as always, Nadja did not disappoint. She seduced my date and tried to convince me to take the two of them home. I explained to her that we were over, but she refused. She took it out on my date, poor girl, never saw it coming. Nadja poured a glass of champagne over her and slapped her in front of two hundred people. I agreed to see her the next day so we could talk and I could make her understand. When we met, though, she said that she was dating someone she had met on location. She agreed that we were over and we left it at that. I was relieved that she had found someone else to focus her attentions on. She just needed to be in control of it, she couldn't let it seem like I had walked away from her, she had to walk away from me. And I was fine with that." He is watching me for a reaction, for anything. But I remain stoic, listening intently.

"I knew she would be back. We started that charity together with my mother when we were teens. I knew we would see each other again, but I was hoping this time, things would change. The time and distance would impact her. I didn't see her again until I started helping Viktor. I told you, she came asking for help the day you came to Miami. I was fresh off the plane when I ran into you that night. Shining in the moonlight with your little white dress and your bare feet, I was spellbound. I had just come from dealing with this woman who pushed me in all the wrong ways. I knew standing in front of her that I would never touch her again. But man, oh man, did I want to touch *you* that night.

When I laid my hand at your back, you bowed into my palm, it was electric. You smelled like salt and strawberries, your skin was so pale and perfect. I wasn't convinced of my own ability to not be a jerk, though, and I didn't want to make the wedding awkward. I didn't want to make the wrong move. But I just couldn't resist. And I am glad that sometimes I have very little self-control, that I give in to my baser urges. I have never felt the kind of connection that I feel with you, Sophie. I cannot stop thinking about you, your voice, your taste, your smell. I need it, I need it all." I fight back a yawn and he lowers his voice. "I am sorry that my past has come back to hurt you, again. But this is it, this is all of me, the good, the bad and the ugly."

"None of it is ugly," I offer, reaching up to wipe my thumb across his lips. "You could never *be* ugly, Rhys. You are too good." I scoot closer to him and try to push myself into his chest, but he holds me back.

"Not tonight," he whispers with a kiss to my head. "You are drunk and angry."

"I am not angry."

"Well, maybe that is because you are drunk, but either way I will not take advantage of you tonight."

"It's not taking advantage if I want it."

"You may say that, but tomorrow you will wake up and you will likely be angry if you remember any of this, and hurting from all those shots. How many did you two have anyway?"

"I don't know, too many."

"Well, you are going to feel them tomorrow."

"I would rather feel something else."

I will see what I can do about that in the morning, but now you need to get some rest. Your eyelids look like they are about to drop like steel doors. This has been a very trying day. Now sleep, Sophie." I drift on a whiskey soaked carpet into a dream state of utter intoxication and twisted images.

Feathers dance across my skin and a lovely light coaxes me from my rest. Flowing across my body like cascades from a gentle waterfall, trails of heat and subtle friction crisscross my body. A warm breeze on my neck travels down my body, over the swell of my breasts and across my bare hips. A slight moan escapes my chest and I am suddenly aware of my sleeping body and the fingers that slide around my curves. I crack my eyes open just a sliver to see Rhys' head sink between my legs.

"Good morning, Beautiful," he purrs before his tongue darts over my clit and I am sprung awake in the most lovely way.

"Rhys, what are you doing?" My voice is hoarse and faint. He peeks from between my thighs and grins.

"You have turned my world upside down. It's only fair I do the same to you." His tongue wraps around my red hot clit and fans the flames. Twisting in tight circles, he laps at my pearl before pulling it into his mouth and sucking me until I scream.

"Oh, my God, you have!" I pant as his lips pop off my clit and blood returns to the rest of my body. A cool breeze rushes over me as he opens me with his fingers. I am hardly awake and yet my body is already in overdrive, throbbing drowsily, a racing pulse slowed only by my heavy, leaden limbs.

Sliding his velvet fingers along my pussy, my core aches, and blood pounds in my veins like a drum line, I cannot hold on any longer. When he slips two fingers into my heat and presses his palm down on my belly, everything in my body that ever has been or ever will be, ignites in a thunderous explosion that rips through me. Violently, my body arches away from the bed, held down only by Rhys' palm, his fingers pump in and out of me as I am torn to shreds and wetness gushes between my legs as he presses hard on my clit.

"I cannot live without you, Sophie," he whispers as his hands coax every ounce of energy from my trembling body. Crash after violent crash rings between my ears as my body is torn apart by the most excruciating ecstasy "I have never felt like this," he pants, working me over. "I never thought I could feel like this." He rushes into me and sinks knuckle deep, cupping my sex in his hand. A mere flick of his finger sets me off again and I scream out, collapsing into his hands. "Yes, Sophie, my God, you are beautiful. Let it go. Let it all go." My legs start to shake as he pumps back into me, swiping across my mons with his warm tongue. I know that I can't take much more, I will surely be torn to shreds and as he lowers his head one last time, I know that I am done for. A quick swipe over my, poor, swollen clit before he spears me with his tongue, lapping at my slick, puffy sex.

The room is filled with the sounds of his tongue rolling across my flesh, his slick fingers pumping my throbbing pussy, and a faint whimper as his fingers glide in a lazy loop. He sucks my swollen nub between his hollow cheeks and presses his palm between my hips again. Every sensation in the world is directed to that small spot, my smoldering core, now a swirling vortex of such intense energy that my body trembles as the last violent explosions ring on high. Tears stream down my face and my body cries out for mercy. My body jerks and seizes as his fingers slip from my folds. I climb the bed, away from him. Too raw, unable to take even the slightest touch. My body crackles and burns while I struggle to gain my breath. My heart races and pounds in my head and I feel completely disconnected. Floating. When I finally open my eyes, his face is lit up with the most amazing, triumphant smile. He reaches out for me and I curl into his arms.

"That was beautiful," he murmurs into my hair, tracing circles on my shoulder with his fingers.

"I think I peed." I peek up at him, mortified and confused.

"No, Sophie, that wasn't pee. That was you coming, harder than ever, and it was hotter than hell. I want to do it again just so I can watch."

"No!" I cry before I can stop myself. "Not all the time. My God! I felt like I was being ripped apart. That was the most intense feeling."

"Then my job here is done." He slaps my ass as he hops from the bed.

"And what was that?" I ask, rolling over, wrapping myself in the soft blue sheets. I watch him stretch his lean body, his arms outstretched, long lengths of muscle pulled taught, his glistening skin tight and smooth.

"To distract you," he grins and I am distracted.

"From what?"

"Your head." He stands at the end of the bed as I sit up. My head throbs like a pounding heart resides in my frontal cortex. Damn Whiskey!

"Ah!" I fall back to the bed and pull the covers up over my head.

"You go ahead and sleep it off, Beautiful. It is still early. I have to go into the office for a couple of hours, tops." He pats my head, under the blankets. I groan and close my eyes, blocking out every sliver of light I can manage. "Will you be alright?"

"Yes," I moan, "just go." I snuggle up into his pillow as I hear the shower roar to life. The scruff on his jaw brushes against my cheek when he kisses me goodbye, coloring my dreams.

Chapter 16

Once I am able to break free from the fog that Rhys left me in, I straighten up the room a bit before heading down to the kitchen, bringing the laptop with me with an idea in mind, but no idea how to execute, or if I really even want to. When I open my email though, the decision is made for me. Greeting me is official bank letterhead and a mountain of legal jargon.The gist being that, the bank will be initiating foreclosure proceedings on my grandmother's house to cover the remainder of her debt. And there it is, staring back at me in black and white. I am losing the very last thing that ties me to anything, anyone, my life, my family. And I know I have to go. By the time Rhys returns, I have already made all the arrangements, knowing that I had to be set before he returned, lest he try and change my mind. When he returns, he finds me upstairs, quietly packing, completely unprepared to face him.

"What are you doing, Beautiful?" He stands in the door, watching shrewdly, and I find it impossible to meet his eyes.

"The bank has started foreclosure proceedings against my grandmother's house. I need to go home and take care of things. I am booked on a flight tonight." I don't want to look him in the face so I occupy myself with packing, tossing random items into my luggage, moving aimlessly between the bathroom and bedroom. The whole time I mill about, he stands, stock still, holding up the door frame as I move through, in and out, not stopping for a touch of his hand, or the brush of his lips. I must keep moving. "My flight leaves at six," I say as I breeze past him again. He reaches out and stops me, swinging me around to meet his pain filled eyes.

"What the fuck are you talking about? Why did you do all of this without talking to me? I was only gone for a couple of hours." I reach up and cup his cheek, his skin is so soft when it's freshly shaved.

"Rhys, it's not a big deal really. I just need to take care of a few things. You knew that I wasn't going to stay here forever. I have a life that I just ran away from and it's still there, waiting for me to return."

"It is a big deal, it's a very big deal, Sophie. You are running." I stop and square my shoulders.

"I am not running."

"Then, I will come with you."

"No. Rhys. You stay here. Please trust me, this is not goodbye, I'm not running away. I just need to go home for a while. I need to settle my grandmother's affairs, I need to face reality. I can't hide here forever." I couldn't possibly tell him that I need some distance, necessary distance between us so I can think straight, and rationally. I am so consumed by him that I am not sure if what I am doing is right. It feels so right most of the time. But when I really stop and think about how I got here, how I came to New York, I was running; running to Rhys just like I ran to Collin. I do not want to do that. I never will be dependent again. I will not be in a situation that I cannot climb out of on my own two feet with my head held high. This is a dangerous scenario with Rhys. I am losing myself, and if I allow myself to fall any further, I know I will never recover.

"It doesn't feel right, Sophie. How long will you be gone?" I don't know the answer to that. If I did it would surely frighten me. With everything that has happened this week, and Olivia's admission, I am confused and running scared.

"I am not sure, I bought a one way ticket. I don't live here, Rhys." The thought of leaving is scary enough, but the thought of never coming back physically hurts. I shake it off. It won't be as serious as that. I just need some space and a little time to clear my head, to think about what I really want, to let the fog lift so I can see clearly again.

"One way?" Breath rushes from his chest as he sits at the edge of the bed looking like he has just had the wind knocked out of him. "Is this about last night? About Nadja? If it is, tell me, tell me so I can fix it. Tell me what I can do to make you stay." I lie as easily as the breath that fills my lungs. I lie through my teeth.

"No, Rhys. It is not about her or any of it. I just need to go home and see to my life."

"Aren't you going to take your watch?"

"I don't know, Rhys, maybe it would be best if I left it here, with you."

"No Sophie, that is a gift for you and I want you to have it. I want you to wear it. Please."

"It's just so…flashy. I feel like I shouldn't accept it."

"Why?" Exasperation and desperation twist through his tone.

"It's too much, Rhys. I have never gotten a gift like this. I don't feel comfortable wearing it."

"Well, it seems I can't do anything right these days," he huffs, stomping down the stairs, leaving me to finish stuffing my bag. I cannot believe that he is being this way. Irritated and strung high on adrenaline, I lose my focus and stand in the middle of the room, searching for my last train of thought, the next task on my to-do list. I am struck by the starkness of the room, for the first time as I look around I notice what is not there. My room is full of my things, pictures and mementos, things that make me feel comfortable. There is nothing here. No defining items, no personal treasures, there is nothing here that says anything about Rhys. And as I take an inventory, I begin to wonder if I really know anything about him.

Nadja was right, I only know what he wants me to know, what he has allowed me to see, until she blew it all out of the water. She forced his hand. The whole situation swirls in my muddled head, the sex, the women, the videos. I knew he had a past, knew he had a reputation. But for brief moments, he felt like he was actually mine. That was *my* scent that wrapped his sweating body after a long session of love making. That was *my* crooked smile, a mere flash and I forget how to breathe. That was *my* hard body pressed against his, our pulses pounding to a private rhythm. But she took it all away. She took what was mine and showed me that it never belonged to me. That it never would. Rhys could no more belong to me than he did to anyone else. She was right. He is a man unto himself and when faced with a bigger, better challenge would surely move swiftly to secure the opportunity.

Who am I kidding? What have I been doing? The sudden threat of losing him for good strangles me and I flit into the bathroom. I don't want him to forget me so easily. It can't all be so flippant and casual. I will stay on his mind, as he will surely be on mine. I spray my gardenia body spray into his top drawer and then over both of his pillows before I zip up my bag and head towards the lion's den. I have to confront him as he tends to his superficial wounds and a bruised ego.

I stand in the doorway and watch him pace like a wild cat. Back and forth over the heavily worn Oriental rug, his feet beat a pattern that is well paced. He links his hands behind his neck and stretches his neck, closing his eyes and suddenly I notice the dark circles. The shadow of exhaustion and unrest is all over him, from his tense shoulders and locked knees to his white knuckles and squared stance. He radiates tension and frustration and I am overcome by the sight of him so clearly out of his comfort zone, so far away from his normal strangle hold on control. It couldn't all stem from me leaving. He slumps down in his chair and lets his heavy fists fall to the desk.

"Damn it," he mutters under his breath before he looks up and catches me watching. "Come here, Beautiful." He pulls me into his orbit, trapping me with his powerful legs. He wraps his arms around my hips and pulls me closer, resting his forehead against my belly. "I really don't want to lose you. What can I do?"

"There is nothing you can do, Rhys. This just isn't about you." He looks up into my eyes, broken. "This is about me. I have to take care of myself. And there is no better time than the present. Please, try to understand that." His hands slide up my back and around my shoulders before he stands and wraps me in his arms. I press my face to his solid chest and listen for the familiar beat of his strong heart. Slow and steady it pounds in his chest, mirroring the rise and fall of his breath. I let my hands slide around his back and across his broad shoulders. A faint moan rumbles in his throat as I run my fingers through his hair and across his neck. His eyes are smoldering as he bends down and presses his candy sweet lips to my waiting mouth.

"You will forgive me, Sophie, if I do not give up so easily. Let's have dinner, put the flight off, just until tomorrow," he whispers, placing a heavy kiss on my shoulder, and another at the base of my throat. "Charlie will pick you up as soon as my meeting is over. We will talk about all of this." He continues to cover me with soft, torturous kisses while breaking down my resolve. "You don't have to leave. We can figure this out together." One last warm kiss behind my ear and his deep green eyes beg for my relent. "Please, Sophie." Our lips meet and a spark startles me, snapping me into the moment. He is smooth, but I am determined, and feel stronger with every kiss that tries to break me down. "Stay." One last whisper. I smile sweetly as he grabs his keys, careful not to answer. "Charlie will be back to pick you up, Sophie. We will handle this. I promise. Trust me."

At four o'clock, I am dressed and ready, one last check in the mirror, one last check of my resolve and I head down to meet the car, and Charlie.

"Hello, Charlie." I love seeing Charlie, he is so genuine and level headed compared to some of the craziness I have encountered in Rhys' circle of friends. He opens the door for me, as the door man loads my bags. I whisper my special request into Charlie's blushing ear and slide an envelope into his hand. "After you drop me off, if you don't mind, Charlie." He looks down on the unmarked envelope and struggles to find a smile. I search his eyes for that loyalty I know is the cornerstone of his personality, and he relents, taking the envelope and tipping his cap, before closing the door behind me.

I sip on my white wine and wait. My hands a restless and my foot taps unbidden at the ground. I am anxious about everything. How do you know you are making the right choice? What if this is a huge mistake? I roll the watch around my wrist, circle after circle, playing with my gift. It is heavy and cold, but it's from Rhys. Right now it is all I have. The rose gold sparkles against my tan skin, my freckles make constellations around the watch face like a sparkling moon, a ring of diamonds circles a shimmering face of blush colored pearl. Hands point at diamond encrusted Roman numerals, and I couldn't tell what time it was if my life depended on it. But it is beautiful. The most generous gift I have ever been given and I am glad to have a piece of Rhys as we lift into the air and I leave New York behind me.

***

"Charlie." Cheeks aflame, he hands me an unmarked envelope in silence, before he scratches his jaw and takes a seat in the booth. I turn the envelope over in my hands, it is not sealed, and there is no doubt where it came from. Her scent wafts from the folded paper within.

"Did Sophie get off safe?" I slug back the remainder of my scotch and gird myself for his explanation. Turning the envelope over in my hand, I do not want to read it for fear that it says, what I know it says. She is gone. She left, I never thought she would really leave.

Shaking his head in confusion, he tries to explain, but there is nothing to be said, she made her choice. I drop my fist to the table with more force than I mean to, knocking the glasses about. Charlie's eyes grow wide and I put my hands up in surrender, in apology, I don't know, in disbelief. She has changed her mind. I don't bother with the envelope or what is inside, I can guess. I stuff it into the inside pocket of my jacket and head for the car with Charlie in tow.

Chapter 17

I took his touch when I left. Ghostly whispers of his finger skating across my heated skin woke me from a deep, unsettling sleep for the first few nights. Melissa also tagged along. Her deep brown eyes mocking me from behind my own lids, her face full of pleasure, her mouth full of rubber.

It took more than a week for the fog to lift. Rhys has that effect on me, a respite that I need to recover from, stripping me of good sense and a strong will. Yet, even as I open my eyes to the rising autumn sun, my mind is shrouded in thoughts of him, his fingers brushing the hair from my face, his lips soft and wet on the curve of my back, his strong hands holding my hips as he plunders my body. I miss him. I reach for my vibrating phone and another sign that I made the wrong choice.

Good Morning, Beautiful. I don't know about you, but I have not been sleeping well, my bed feels so empty without you, my house so cold. Although I have tried to do as you wish, I find my desire for you cannot be denied. You are the one thing in this life that has allowed me the possibility of being something different, someone different. I would be a fool to let you go, it would be to abandon the very possibility of my better self.

A variation of the same message, every morning since I left. I thought being away from him would afford me a little clarity, that I would discover in the bright light of a Rhys free day that I didn't really need him, that it was all contrived, not real. But it is real. It is so real I can taste his skin on my tongue. I hear his voice in my dreams. This is real. And suddenly I want to drop everything and run. Run back to New York, back into his arms and apologize. Apologize for leaving, forever thinking that I could fight this, for ever denying that I needed him.

I sit up and call him immediately.

"Good Morning, Beautiful." His warm voice slides through the phone and he comes rushing back into my bloodstream. Like a shot of adrenaline, my heart beats stronger and I am alive again. I didn't realize how much I missed him, missed that voice. I need to hear him, for him to call me Beautiful every day. I want to go back.

"Good morning," the softest whisper before my voice cracks.

"I miss you, Sophie."

"I miss you, too."

"I want you to come back, and stay, in New York. Please, come back." Tears swell in my eyes and I take a deep, cleansing breath. The deepest breath I have taken in ages and all at once I am full and so empty.

"Rhys."

"Sophie," he cuts me off, "I love you." My heart stops and my life in *loves* flashes quickly behind my eyes. I am acutely aware that no *love* has ever felt like that, like the all-consuming comfort of a warm flame that you know won't harm you, the slow sweet flow of honey that coats your throat. His love is all I have ever needed. He just filled me up, just like that, three little words that I have heard a million times, but never really felt, until now. My tongue is limp in my mouth, my mind raging so loudly that I cannot hear a thing. This man loves me! This man loves me, me. Sophie. I don't know how long the silence lasts as I contemplate the prize I have just been given. My mind races to catch up and the last few months flash before me. How much has changed. How full and open my heart feels, like a rolling meadow with no end in sight my feelings for him know no horizon. No ending, I will surely swell and burst.

"I love you, too!" I cannot get the words out fast enough, I am bursting.

"Jesus, Beautiful, that felt amazing. Say it again."

"I love you." I reply with a smile that I know he can hear, as I can hear his. The tilt of his grin, the crinkle in his eyes, I can feel it in my heart. I fucking love this man. And he loves me.

"Come back." A quiet, but forceful demand that I will gladly fulfill.

"I want to. I will."

"Today."

"Rhys, I have some things that have to be taken care of. Today, I have a meeting at the bank, liquidating everything I own to try and save my grandmother's house. I have to finish packing up all her stuff. I am almost done, I promise."

"I don't want to wait, Sophie. I fucking need you in my arms right now." The urgency is palpable in his voice, his tone colored now with anxiety and impatience.

"Tomorrow. I think I can be done with everything and be ready to go by tomorrow."

"Let's shoot for tonight," he quickly replies. I hear a muffled voice in the background and the distinct sound of a hand covering the phone, before he returns. "Sophie, my love." The words settle heavily between us, pulling us together. "I have a few meetings this morning and lunch with my father and then I will call you. Do you think you will be at the bank by then?"

"My appointment is at noon."

"Okay, Beautiful, I want you to call me as soon as you finish at the bank, and we will make all the arrangements. I cannot stand the idea of another night away from you. I need you, Sophie. I need you now." If it was possible to overdose on happiness I would surely be a writhing pile of limbs on the floor right now. My heart feels so full that it could burst in my chest and my lips are on the verge of cracking from the force of a smile the likes I have never experienced. I am done. This is it.

"Yes, Rhys, I will call you."

"I can't wait, Sophie. I cannot wait to tell you I love you in person. I need to see your face, Beautiful. It's killing me not to see you. You have made me so happy. I have to run, until later, my love."

"I love you," I reply before he is abruptly gone, and I am left to my pounding heart and love fogged mind.

The morning slips away in a jumble of busy work and day dreaming. Floating away and wasting time with Rhys, locked in a room until neither of us can take another moment. Working as hard as I can with such a consuming distraction on my mind. After I sign my life away at the bank, I treat myself to lunch from the dollar menu. Such is my life now. And I head to my grandmother's house to pack the last few boxes. I wait to call Rhys, giving myself an hour. An hour to get as much done as possible, knowing as soon as we speak, the wheels will be in motion. When I finally come up for air, I find my phone rattling away on the kitchen counter. Twenty five missed calls. And it jumps to life in my hand.

"Sophie! Where have you been? I have been trying to reach you forever!"

"I have been at the bank, signing away every penny I have or ever will have, to try and save Lola's house. And now I am packing. Why? What is going on?"

"Rhys…" She hangs his name out, breathes, and leaves it hanging. "He was in an accident, Sophie. He and Michael."

"What?" The breath rushes from my chest, replaced by a tangible, strangling panic. A panic so virile I can taste it. I have been here before.

"He and Michael were in a car accident. You should get here, Sophie. It's serious." The panic in her voice pushes me over the precipice. My heart drops to the floor. A dead thud fills my head. My knees give way and I sink to the cold, hard tile.

"Sophie, are you still there?" The phone suddenly feels like dead weight. Lead in my hand. I struggle to bring it back to my ear.

"I'm still here," I manage, choking on grief.

"You need to get here fast." I look down at my wrist, and the sparkling, over the top gift. The icy cold, heavy watch that Rhys insisted upon buying. *The gift of time,* he quipped. The only thing I own of any worth. The only thing I own now, of any value, real personal value. I have to get to him.

***

The flight, the cab ride, everything is a blur. I am numb and exhausted. The only thing I feel is the urgent pull to get to the hospital, to get to him. I need to tell him I am sorry. I need to tell him the truth.

The hum and chaos of the city can't even touch me. I see New York through the window, passing by, teeming with life. Cars weave and bob past us, horns blaring but I hear none of it. Throngs of people flow up and down packed sidewalks, crossing traffic in waves, I don't see a single face. All I can see is my past flashing before my eyes, the searing, white hot pain and anticipation of losing everything.

We pull up to Mt. Sinai and I am frozen. Stuck in the sticky, worn, back seat, my eyes scale the ominous black tower rising from the center of the hospital. The cab driver bangs on the partition, demanding his fare and my exit. I pull what cash I have left from my hastily packed purse and push a twenty through the slot. He laughs, a deep chortle, before he begins to yell in a language I do not understand. Banging his chubby fist on the partition, he stabs his short dirty fingers at the meter. He is animated and exasperated, the meter reads $64.20. God damn, this city is going be the death of me, and my meager pockets.

The city is stagnant. Humidity hangs in the September air like a shroud. Coating everything in an exhaust filled, grimy mist. Never have I been so assaulted by my surroundings. Turning my eyes to the dark night sky, caught in the looming shadow of the sleek, black tower, I imagine Rhys, lying in that prophetic building. Please, don't let me be too late! I hear my name, carried on a hot breeze, and it feels like a bad dream. I turn towards the entrance when Olivia appears, as if out of thin air.

"Sophie! You're here, thank God." Dazed and caught off guard, I grab her arm to steady me.

"Um….yeah. I am here." She holds me at arm's length, headlights flash across her eyes and she shakes her head.

"Sophie, I know Rhys would want you here, but you cannot go in there now."

"What? Why?" Inside, I am pushing past her, rushing to Rhys' side. I look down to find my feet anchored to the dirty sidewalk, as Olivia stands before me with an all too familiar grief in her eyes.

"Listen to me. He is in really bad shape. They have him in an induced coma. But his mother and Nadja are up there. I cannot let you go in there. They are chomping at the bit, and they will eat you alive. Rhys would not want that, and neither do I."

"But…What? Why is she here? What am I supposed to do?"

"Matthew is in there with them. He will keep us posted, and let us know as soon as they leave. There is nothing we can do for him now anyhow."

"Olivia.." My voice cracks as I wipe away the first heavy tear, I held it at bay as long as I could. "What if it's too late?"

"It won't be. They are doing everything they can. He is in very capable hands." She pulls me toward a waiting Town Car, the driver casually leaning on the hood watching our exchange. He scrambles to open the back door as Olivia gives him a signal. "Come, let's get you settled, and we will wait for word from Matthew."

"Settled?" I yank my hands from hers, angry, frustrated and quickly sinking into an abyss. It's all too much, our petty squabble, the accident, his mother, and Nadja. I came all the way here just to be turned away? I cannot stand the thought of him lying there alone. But the thought of Nadja being at his side stokes a distracting, if not comforting rage. "Where are we going?" I don't want to go anywhere. I want to plant myself at the hospital, at Rhys' side. His mother and Nadja be damned! The car pulls out, seamlessly blending into the heavy traffic. Olivia squeezes my hand, pulling my attention from the disappearing hospital.

"You will come and stay with me and Matthew." She holds her hand in the air, cutting off my inevitable protest. "Stop, I won't hear anything about it. I am doing this for you, and you are going to let me. I am just so sorry this is happening."

The remainder of the ride is silent. The sound of my pounding heart and my racing pulse drown out Olivia and the rest of the city.

Me

If I give you – those pieces of me
Would you care – for us like me
And think the world – belongs to me
I'd leave no corner – unearthed by me
To give the love – that resides in me

~ Darcy

Watch for more Rhys and Sophie in *Shout*
The final installment of The Voice Trilogy

Keep up with Noelle:
Email: noellebodhaine@gmail.com
Facebook : www.facebook.com/noellebodhaine
Pinterest: n.bodhaine
Twitter @noellebodhaine
Goodreads : Noelle Bodhaine
Instagram: @noellebodhaine